Tattered Promises

The Shards of Promise, Volume 1

Tori Lennox

Published by Tori Lennox, 2023.

TATTERED PROMISES

First edition. March 30, 2023.

Copyright © 2023 Tori Lennox.

ISBN: 978-0999460443

Written by Tori Lennox.

To My Readers, Thank you for letting me share the stories in my head.

PROLOGUE

Northumberland, England

"Davi!"

Ignoring the shout of her assistant from across the field, Davida sat back on her haunches and rested her palms on her thighs.

"Davi!"

Studying the bony protuberance, she silently acknowledged the skull staring back at her. No, not the skull. Wulfgar. His name was Wulfgar. She'd just spent the past three hours reverently picking dirt from around *Wulfgar's* skull.

"Davi!"

Shaking her head, Davida briefly wondered what had Leslie's knickers in a knot this time. Likely a trustee flexing their muscles. If she ignored them, they'd call back at a more convenient time. They always did. Right now, she didn't have time for frivolous interruptions. Not when she was on the cusp of a major discovery.

While she didn't know much more than she had when she started, she did know this skull was male. While not yet verified, she was confident they'd found their first Angle warrior of the season. If she wasn't mistaken, that bit of metal glinting by bony phalanges was the pommel of a sword or the hilt of a dagger. She'd know more when Jodi finished excavating her square.

What she did know from Wulfgar's grave goods was that he was a man of means. The garnet cloisonné belt buckle discovered a couple of days ago supported that theory. As did the imported glassware and pottery littering the grave. However,

Wulfgar, while wealthy, wasn't royal. They hadn't found any of the ceremonial accoutrements anywhere.

More likely, he was a pagan warband leader who died on the battlefield. Glimpses of long-healed cuts and unhealed fractures lent credence to that argument. They'd know more when they did a full examination. Maybe they'd discover his cause of death.

Ignoring Leslie screeching in the background, she stared at the half-exposed skeleton waiting to be uncovered, cataloged, and respectfully carried to the workroom before adding a few scribbles to her clipboard. The first thing she noted was that Wulfgar was tall for the 6th or 7th century. Tall and heavily muscled as only a farmer-warrior could be. He likely had a family, friends, and followers who mourned his passing. People who cared enough to bury him with the ceremony befitting his station in life. Imagining the grieving burial party, she felt a hint of sorrow at their loss.

Shaking her emotions, Davida refused to get mired in Wulfgar's humanity when she had work to do. The excavation needed to be photographed, sketched, and recorded. She could spin evocative scenarios for the media after the grunt work was done. Right now, she had to record her first impressions while the body was in situ. Things like noting how deeply his bones were buried and sketching the patterns on those fragments of textile Leslie photographed earlier. There would be time to assemble the puzzle when they had all the pieces. So far, they'd barely opened the box.

Staring at the skull, Davida decided Wulfgar's face was well-formed with sharp cheekbones and a strong jaw. His hair was dark blonde from the strands still stubbornly clinging to his crown. Stepping out on a mental limb, she'd surmise his eyes were green, grey, or blue, and his complexion lightly tanned. Then again, he could be a dark-eyed brunette. It wouldn't be the first time that hair color was altered by some natural agent in the soil. She'd know more after further testing.

Setting her clipboard aside, Davida smiled softly. The face forming in her mind was strong and attractive. Entirely too close for comfort to a face she'd rather forget. Shaking her thoughts, she silently mocked her flights of fancy. Treating Wulfgar's remains with dignity didn't include imaginary imaginings. It certainly didn't involve thoughts about *him*.

Getting back to business, she wouldn't know how accurate her impressions were until they did the DNA and facial reconstruction. Snorting softly, she admitted that wouldn't happen for a while. If at all. She didn't have the final say on that. The trustees did, and they could be tight with the purse strings. She didn't blame them. Not really. Not if they wanted the funding to last. Unnecessary expenses were often axed in favor of prudence. While their pockets were very deep, they weren't bottomless.

Taking a sip of water, Davida hopped back in the trench, prepared to get back to work. Staring at her vast assortment of tools, she laughed softly, realizing she'd used everything from trowels to dental picks to wooden sculpting tools to plastic spoons and brushes in her quest to carefully expose Wulfgar's near-perfect skull.

The quicker he was freed from his grave, the quicker they could begin figuring out who and what, he was. Halting at the sound of Leslie's now desperate tone, she finally looked up to see her assistant running towards her with her cell in hand. Climbing out of the trench, she met the woman halfway.

"What's up?" she hoped it wasn't funding or paperwork related. "I don't have time to give gratuitous updates."

It wasn't time yet. While she was mostly left alone thanks to quarterly updates in London, every few weeks she'd get a call from one trustee or another reminding her who held the purse strings. As distasteful as she'd found the posturing in the beginning, she'd quickly learned to roll with it.

The ridiculous reminders of who wielded power were a necessary evil, and she was a lucky girl. As long as she kept her eye on the prize, she could tolerate the intolerable. She could and she would, for very good reasons.

Not every archaeological dig was as well-funded as Deira. Most weren't. While she was grateful for the Shuttleworths' generosity, continually jumping through hoops to satisfy bureaucratic egos grew tedious a long time ago. However, while not pleasant, never having to worry about money was worth the silly mind games.

"You'll take this call." Leslie handed her the cell. "It's your stepmother."

"Marti?" Davida spoke into the phone. "What's wrong?"

Watching Leslie prepare to walk away, she motioned for her to stay. From the sound of things, this conversation was heading south in ways that seriously impacted her life and her dig. Her assistant needed to be here from the start.

"Calm down." Her stepmother was losing it across four thousand miles. Truthfully, she'd probably lost it a while ago when she refused to answer Leslie's summons. While understandable, she'd never get anything done if she kowtowed to every unnecessary call; under the current circumstances, her delay was unforgivable. "I'll catch the first flight out. Yes, I agree. It's our little secret. Dad will never know you called."

Right. Like her father wouldn't see through that lie five seconds after she arrived in his hospital room unannounced. Her stepmother was a ditz at times. Shaking her head in disbelief, Davida ended the call and spoke a few words into her cell. "Give me a minute."

Saying a silent prayer of thanks that her connection held long enough to make the necessary arrangements, Davida closed her eyes and gathered her thoughts. The past few minutes were a rare miracle. Cell service around the dig was spotty at best. Nonexistent at worst. Stuffing her phone in her pocket, Davida turned to Leslie.

"I'm sorry." She looked at her assistant. "I have to go home. My Dad had a heart attack. Marti claims it's bad. How bad, I don't know. The woman's hysterical."

"Then go, we'll take care of this." Leslie motioned to the trench. "I'm assuming you just booked your flight and a rental car?"

"I did." Davida verified. "I have just long enough to brief everyone and swing by the house to pack a bag before I have to be at the airport."

"Then I'll drive you." Her boss was in no condition to be behind the wheel.

"Thanks." Davida headed towards their headquarters. "We can discuss the site on the drive."

"You don't have anything to worry about," Leslie stated what they both knew. "We know what to do while you're gone, and how to contact you when we don't. You just need to take care of your family."

"Thanks for being the best assistant in the world," Davida gave the highest praise she could. "Things wouldn't run nearly as well without you. All I can say is call me if you need me, and the site's all yours."

"Sounds good." Cupping her hands around her mouth, Leslie's loud whistle urged the stragglers to join the rest of the group already forming around the meeting table. "Let's get this show on the road."

Once her team was assembled, Davida filled them in on her father's illness. Accepting their good wishes, she informed everyone she would return as soon as possible. Until then, the site was Leslie's. What she said went, end of story.

While not expected, she was grateful no one protested the temporary change in leadership. Her team was a well-oiled machine thanks to the fact that they'd worked together for years. Except for a few volunteers, they were all at Deira before she was, which meant everyone knew their place and they were happy in it. She didn't have to contend with the constant jockeying for position she'd endured on other digs.

Exhaling wearily, Davida was glad she'd had the wisdom to follow in her predecessor's footsteps. Doc had a way with people she'd tried to emulate. That meant she shared credit for their finds with everyone and ensured her people knew how much their diverse talents and experience were valued. They needed each other to get the job done, and they knew it. For all her easygoing ways, she ran a tight ship. Narcissism and drama were not tolerated.

"You ready?"

"Yeah."

Falling in step with Leslie, Davida quickly dialed her stepmother to let her know she'd booked her flight and a rental car. Telling Marti she'd drive straight to the hospital from the airport, she expected to hang up only to find herself bombarded with the other woman's fears instead.

Reassuring her stepmother that her father was much too young and healthy to die, Davida realized this was the most she'd talked to the woman since the day she married her father. It wasn't like they had a lot in common. They didn't. Nothing except their love for David.

Wrapping up the conversation, she couldn't help thinking that, despite her confident reassurances, heart attacks were serious. Her father could die. Just hopefully not before she saw him one last time and cleared the air between them.

CHAPTER ONE

A tlanta, Georgia, USA
Pulling her bag across the parking lot to the black
SUV, Davina tossed her suitcase and carry-on into the backseat
of her rental. She was running much later than she wanted. Not
unexpectedly, it had taken forever to clear customs and grab
her baggage. Forget the line to collect this beauty. Sliding into
the driver's seat, she rested her forehead against the steering
wheel. She was insanely tired, and she couldn't deny that any
longer.

An unplanned international flight with no sleep did that to
a girl, especially when she'd spent the past three days digging
in the dirt. She probably had grit under her fingernails if she
stopped to look. She wouldn't. Marti's call had galvanized her
into action. She couldn't rest until she saw her father. She
couldn't risk anything happening before they had the conversation she'd spent half a decade avoiding.

Taking a deep breath, she dreaded the day had finally come.
While she knew she couldn't avoid the talk forever, she never
expected it to come so soon or in this way. She always thought
she'd wake up one day and it wouldn't hurt anymore. When
that happened, she'd know it was time to tell her father why
she'd left so suddenly and never looked back.

Unfortunately, it seemed she was wrong. How she'd imagined the scenario wasn't how it was. Yesterday, she was on a
different continent doing what she loved best. Now, she was
where she'd vowed never to be again. Sitting up, Davida railed
against events beyond her control. Her dad could be dead for

all she knew. She hoped not. She prayed not. She'd come too far to bury him with no goodbye.

Sighing, she acknowledged she felt more like the parent than the child. What else was new? Her father's crazy antics had landed him in hot water more than once, so she was glad when he finally remarried. While not wild about his bride, she was grateful for Marti's calming effect. It seemed her gratitude was premature.

David had done something to cause his heart attack. She knew it. She didn't know why. She just did. Maybe because she felt the familiar dread in the pit of her stomach that she'd felt so many times before. That sense of anxiety that screamed something wasn't right and her father was at the epicenter.

It wouldn't surprise her if that was true. David was a jovial, larger-than-life character hiding his brilliance beneath a jester's cap. One who liked skirting too close to the precipice. She suspected he'd miscalculated the distance to the edge this time. He may have skidded over. However, she wouldn't know until she saw him.

Sitting up, she pulled out of her parking space and headed for the interstate. Like it or not, she had a long drive across town to reach her hotel. But the hospital was closer. As tired as she was, maybe she should visit her dad before she checked in. Once she did, she could gratefully yield to the lure of a comfortable bed.

She also needed to call her team back home. While she trusted her underlings to hold down the fort, this was the worst possible time to abandon her dig. Not only were they nearing the end of the season, but they were on the cusp of making the biggest discovery of her career.

Unfortunately, that didn't matter. Deira was on hold for the next few days. She had to come home, and she had to do it now. From what she'd gleaned from Marti's hysteria, her father's situation was dire. Knowing that, she couldn't stay away. If something happened without her presence, she would never forgive herself.

As for her dig, Davida was confident with every passing day that her team had discovered an unknown royal settlement. One that dated to the late 6th or early 7th century. If her supposition proved true, her team would help flesh out a period of Anglo-Saxon history that was sorely lacking in concrete information.

Shaking her head, she was torn between her loyalty to her family and her loyalty to work. She was also torn between hoping Leslie would halt their forward progress until her return and hoping she didn't. Since she'd left her crew with little instruction to catch that last-minute flight from Newcastle to Atlanta, the next move was up to them.

Pulling into the hospital parking lot, Davida was surprised by how fast she'd arrived at her destination. Glancing at the clock, she acknowledged she'd been lost in thought far longer than she realized. There was something about holding that exquisite Anglo-Saxon belt buckle in her hand that still haunted her. She'd envisioned the mighty Angle warrior who'd once worn it without even trying. She still saw him in her mind.

Abandoning her romantic imaginings, Davida focused on the present instead. Slicking a neutral gloss over her lips, she checked her reflection in the rearview mirror, smoothed her hair, and exited the car. Like it or not, she had to confront her father. Whether he leveled with her was another story.

TATTERED PROMISES

Walking through the sliding glass doors, she quickly found the elevators and made her way to the sixth floor. She found herself entering her father's room much too soon. Expecting to see her stepmother, she was surprised to find herself face to face with her father, hanging onto his IV pole for dear life.

"Davi, what are you doing here?" Stepping back, David motioned her into the room. "I told Marti not to call you."

"I'll just bet you did." Davida rolled her eyes. "Seriously? You thought she would listen? You had a heart attack."

"Mild," David informed her as he sat on the edge of his bed. "Stress induced." A reluctant admittance. "There are no blockages and minimal damage. My heart is strong. I'm only here for observation and rest."

There was more to the story than he was telling. She could see it in his eyes. Besides, she knew him too well to accept his words at face value. Her dad never volunteered anything that wasn't necessary. That was just his way. All she could do at this point was wait him out and waste precious time she didn't have. Taking a seat by his bed, Davida settled in for the long haul.

"So, other than the heart attack, how are you?" While making small talk was the last thing she wanted, it was the only way to get to the bottom of what happened. "How is Marti holding up?"

Listening to her father drone on about insignificant things, Davida prayed he would slip up and reveal something that was. Until he did, there was no way she could return home. Not when she knew this was but the tip of the iceberg. One that she was positive would bite her in the rear somewhere down the road, as his transgressions usually did.

"So, Marti's at home getting rest?" Davida leaned back in her chair. "I'm sure I'll see her before I leave. Why don't you lie down before you fall? You look better than I expected, but still green around the gills."

"Thanks." David laughed at her understatement. "I don't know how bad you expected me to look, but I know I look like hell. I do have eyes, you know."

"Beautiful eyes," Davida agreed. "I thought you were taking better care of yourself, considering you have a hot young wife at home."

"While I'm sure Marti would love to hear herself called hot, I have a lot more than my wife to live for." David reached out to take her hand. "I have you as well, and I have been taking care of myself. I just had a physical two months ago. I checked out fine. This came out of left field without warning."

"That happens sometimes, I guess." Right, not with her dad. "It's been a while since I've been home."

"Five years." About four and a half years past a while in his book. "You look beautiful. A little thinner and more strawberry than when you left."

The more vibrant color looked good on his girl, as did her thick, shoulder-length locks. Studying her appearance, David admitted his daughter was a pretty woman with her big blue eyes, even features, and pouty lips. She always had been. But time and experience had matured her beyond mere youthful prettiness.

She now had a touch of that confident swagger women get when they make it to the top of a man's field. Smiling at the thought, David acknowledged his baby girl was at the top, and she'd made it in record time. Too bad his boss wasn't around to appreciate the change. It was kind of sexy. Or it would be if he weren't her doting father.

"Your mom would be so proud of you." David praised. "I'm proud of you. While I'm sorry about what happened, leaving this place allowed you to spread your wings in ways you never could have if you stayed. You proved yourself a remarkable woman."

"I guess I did." Davida agreed. "I certainly wouldn't be where I am professionally speaking."

At best, she would have worked local digs like her mother. At worst, her dreams would have been sacrificed on the altar of marriage and motherhood until her kids were older. Considering she'd always wanted a family, she would have been content with her life. She knew that.

However, she would have missed the fantastic opportunities she'd experienced over the past few years. While the girl she was wouldn't have missed the life she never knew, the woman she'd become didn't regret the detours her life had taken.

"No, you wouldn't," David agreed. "Luce said you'd make it big. I wasn't sure, but she knew from the time you were small."

"I guess she did." Hearing her mother believed in her meant more than her father knew. "Why don't you catch me up on everything I've missed while I was gone?"

It was time to steer the conversation into safer waters. Before her father shared why he didn't think she'd ever follow her dreams. She knew it had something to do with the man she'd left behind. She didn't want to talk about failed marriages or estranged husbands. Neither had any place in her life today.

"I can do that." David turned his head to look at her. "After you tell me about your latest dig."

She'd forgotten how good he was at deflection.

"Why don't I do that?" There was no reason to fight him; she wouldn't win. "The most important thing we're working on right now is trying to figure out if we've stumbled onto a royal tun. Every discovery reveals a bit more we didn't know. The whole thing is like putting a giant puzzle together one tiny piece at a time."

Seeing the way her eyes lit up as she described the Angle warrior's skeleton they'd recently discovered told David he didn't have to worry about her uncovering the newest skeleton in his closet any time soon. If all went to plan, she'd be back in Yorkshire, buried in her dig long before his sins caught up with him. If it didn't, all hell would break loose.

CHAPTER TWO

E scaping to her rental car, Davida sighed wearily as she slid into the driver's seat. Dealing with her father was never easy. Especially when she was already done. She'd regaled him with every interesting anecdote she could remember, hoping he'd open up in turn. He hadn't. He shared little more than the fact that Marti now worked at a different school. That, and he was thinking about buying a new car as soon as he finished his due diligence. If she thought something was off before, she knew it was now.

Leaning back in her seat, she reached for her cell, wondering what her team needed now. The thought that they were ringing so soon made her uneasy. Everything was running smoothly when she left. What could have possibly happened in less than a day? Answering the call, she was shocked to hear a masculine voice she hadn't heard in five long years. She was stunned, but not surprised, that he had her number. Where there was a will, there was a way. When that will came with an influential name and deep pockets, mountains crumbled.

Enduring small talk for courtesy's sake, Davida finally gave in. If Jensen wanted to see her, she'd indulge him. He'd waited five years for the pleasure. Hopefully, playing nice would get her what she wanted, and this conversation would end with the d-word. With any luck, he'd already have the papers waiting on his desk. Since divorce was the next logical step after their long separation, she'd happily sign on the dotted line if the terms were equitable.

Pulling out of the hospital parking lot, she drove across town to the familiar office building. The area had grown in her absence. Developed, but not improved from what she saw around her. Pulling into a well-lit space near the door, she absorbed her surroundings.

It was late enough that the parking lot was deserted except for the desperate few seeking to climb the corporate ladder. Too bad they never would. Not with Blake Enterprises. Jensen promoted on ability, not willingness to work long hours. The only overtime his best employees put in was when he did, too.

Stopping by the security desk, Davida flashed her driver's license before entering the elevator. While the young man wasn't familiar, she was pleased to see from the lobby photos that Bobby was still head of security. She would have to see him before she left. Right now, she had a cranky lion to beard in his opulent den.

Arriving at the familiar office, Davida snorted cynically when the door opened before she could knock. Jensen was always one step ahead of the game. Entering his lair, she suppressed a growl. Who got better-looking with age? Her soon-to-be ex, that's who. It was so unfair. Saying the past few years had been kind to him was an understatement.

While she'd added a few demeaning freckles across the bridge of her nose, he'd prematurely added a light sprinkle of white through his ebony mane and a striking air of distinction he didn't need. Casting her worst half a snarky look, Davida tossed herself into one of the massive leather wing chairs with the same long-limbed nonchalance she affected when they were together. It was all an act. There was no way in heaven or hell she'd let him see how anxious she felt.

16

TATTERED PROMISES

"Long time no see, but I have other places to be, so what do you say we cut to the chase?" Davida smirked at the imperiously quirked brow, amused that her estranged husband was unwittingly channeling his judgmental father. "Hey, I'm being expedient. Neither of us has time to dance around the issues."

"No, we don't," Jensen agreed. "My dad's given us five years to work things out. Now he's done with it. As far as Dan is concerned, it's time to reconcile and start that family we always wanted."

"Not just no." Davida barked as she abruptly lunged at his desk. "Hell no." Her father-in-law had officially flipped his lid. "I came here expecting to sign divorce papers; not hear some crazy crap your daddy said."

Jensen cocked a brow, unsurprised his wife hadn't mellowed over the years. Well-mannered in public, in private, the woman was feisty on a good day and impossible on a bad one.

While pleased she'd remained the same, he wasn't in the mood to argue. He had a need only she could fill, and Dan had given him the leverage to make her. Opening his mouth to speak, Davida cut him off instead.

"You need to know something before this goes one word further." She leaned on his desk and glared at him. "We started that family five years ago." She barreled ahead, ignoring the disbelief on his face. "I was seven weeks pregnant when that photograph broke."

Feeling unexpected tears well, she rushed through what she needed to say.

"I miscarried that night, so don't mention the family we always wanted. We had it, we lost it, we're done. Blake Enterprises has no further claim on my womb."

Turning on her heel, Davida headed for the door only to find her arm grabbed by the much larger male.

"Not just no." Jensen tossed her words back at her. "Hell no. You don't say something like that and flounce out the door."

"Fine, you've got five minutes to say what you need to say." Davida glanced at her watch. "The clock's ticking."

"Then have a seat." Jensen escorted her back to her chair before settling back behind his desk as though he hadn't just taken a verbal punch to the gut. "We need to talk. Let's start with the fact that tidbit is something you should have shared five years ago. That baby was my child, too."

Emotions aside, her admission complicated an already complicated situation. While he understood her reluctance to give him a second chance, he was more determined than ever to complete his mission. He'd always wanted a life and a family with this woman, and he intended to have one. He just wasn't sure how to go about convincing her that she wanted the same. Especially given this latest bombshell.

"I didn't think you'd care," Davida said calmly. "You were with someone else."

"I wasn't with anyone but you." Jensen wanted to yell at her stupidity, but restrained himself. "Not like that."

"You could have fooled me." Davida was startled by the venom in her tone. "Sharon was all over you."

"Not for long," Jensen corrected. "And I wasn't all over her at all. I didn't invite her to dinner that night, and I didn't invite her to kiss me." He fought to keep his voice even. "I also never reciprocated. It was an engineered photo op to advance her career. One I never saw coming. I would have told you that if you'd confronted me instead of dropping off the face of the earth."

"She didn't kiss you." She wouldn't have liked it, but she could have eventually blown that off. "She was on your lap with her hand down your pants."

That alone should have told her something was seriously off. For one thing, he wasn't into overt PDA's. Forget anything so graphic. They'd never indulged in more than casual hugs, handholding, and genteel good-bye kisses, and they were married. It wasn't their style. Behind closed doors was another matter. While the specifics might vary, the conclusion never did. His wife's innate sensuality put Sharon's practiced skills to shame.

"While I can't deny what you saw," Jensen snorted softly. "I can tell you, contrary to popular belief, her overture didn't ellicit an automatic sexual response. Sharon was the last thing I wanted."

He'd sampled her wares enough in the past to know he wasn't interested in anything she had to offer. Besides, he'd known her daring was more about publicity than a real invitation back into her bed. While she would if he would, she hadn't expected him to take her up on her offer, and he hadn't.

"Whatever." Davida huffed. "You were still somewhere you shouldn't be."

"I was in New York on business." Jensen reminded her. "You know it's not uncommon to work out the final details of a deal over dinner and a drink at the club. That's what happened that night."

Davida's mutinous expression didn't change. While his words were true, it didn't change anything.

"We completed the deal, shared a celebratory brandy, and everyone left but me. I had a few minutes until my car arrived, so I used the time to update my dad and my assistant. I didn't know Sharon was in town until she plopped down beside me and made her move."

"You didn't know she photographed everything?" There was nothing she could say to that.

"Not until I came home to an empty house to find that gossip rag and your wedding rings on the counter." It had taken several days for the truth to penetrate through the shock that she'd left in the first place. "You should have confronted me with what you thought you knew. We could have worked through everything."

Without losing the last five years of their lives and their relationship.

"Maybe, but I wasn't in any condition to confront you for a long time." She was too hurt and angry to even contemplate it. "That's why my lawyer handled everything for me."

"I never cheated on you back then." He wished he could say the same now, but they both knew better. "I hope you know that."

"What I knew didn't matter," Davida reminded him. "How it looked, did, and that was devastating. Don't forget you were engaged to that skank before we met. What was I supposed to think?"

Especially considering she'd been a geeky, middle-class kid way out of her depth, while Sharon was a wealthy, experienced woman used to the high society scene.

"I never hid our involvement," Jensen reminded her. "However, I wasn't the one who broke things off. Sharon did. She had the opportunity to hook a bigger fish, and she took it. Do you honestly believe I'd rekindle a relationship with the woman who left me at the altar?"

One he'd never loved in the first place, even if she passed his mother's sniff test. Despite Tara's seal of approval, Sharon had undesirable qualities as well. Ones she'd used to trick the woman he truly loved into leaving him. While he could forgive a lot, that was unforgivable.

"With hindsight, no," Davida reluctantly admitted. "At the time, I wasn't thinking clearly."

"Then you have your answer." Jensen stared her down. "You should have told me."

"Maybe I should have, but I didn't," Davida agreed. "You should have contacted me after the fact."

"I tried," Jensen answered honestly. "I couldn't get through your wall of protectors. Now I know why."

"That was probably true for the first year or so," Davida agreed. "But you never contacted me after the separation papers were signed. Why now?"

"I told you why." Deciding they needed a tension breaker, Jensen opened the bottle of wine a satisfied client had left earlier in the day and poured two small glasses. "My father has lost his mind."

"I agree." Davida stared into her wine glass before taking a hearty sip. "Expecting you to settle down and have a child in a year is rather extreme."

"He'll extend it to two years," Jensen informed her. "If I'm trying." He shook his head at his father's audacity. "After that, all bets are off. I lose everything."

Her look said she doubted that.

"Davi, that includes the company I've run successfully for the past six years. As far as Dan is concerned, I'm over forty with nothing to show for myself but a healthy bank account and a dissipated lifestyle."

He was barely forty-two.

"Surely he doesn't believe that?"

Of all the things she could say about her husband, he wasn't a player. Not really. Who cared if he'd had several long-term relationships and a broken engagement behind him before they met? He was a wealthy, desirable man. He was as much the pursued as the pursuer. But he'd never been a lowlife even when she'd believed the worst of him.

"Dan should know you better."

"He should," Jensen agreed. "He doesn't. Not really. He was happily married with three rambunctious kids by the time he was my age. He can't get his mind around what happened between us."

They were happy; then they weren't.

"How could he?" Jensen's intense stare was accusatory. "I didn't understand myself."

He did now, but that didn't ease his heartbreak or change his circumstances.

"I'm sorry you're in this mess." Dan wasn't the most reasonable man at the best of times. "I hope you have a woman in mind. Have the papers sent to my hotel room. I'll have my attorney look them over before I sign. If there's an issue, I'll let you know. That's the best I can do for you."

"No, you won't, and it isn't." Jensen reached for her hand. "I meant what I said. I expect us to reconcile as soon as you can arrange it."

"And I meant what I said." Davida's stare said he'd lost his mind. "Not just no, but hell no."

"I didn't want to do this, but you're forcing my hand." Jensen forged ahead, ignoring the disbelief on her face. "You don't have a choice. We either reconcile, or David is arrested for embezzlement. Your father has stolen a quarter million dollars from the company since you left."

He'd taken double that, but Davida didn't need to know the ugly truth. It would wreck her life more than he already had. She adored her father. She'd blame herself.

"You're lying." Davida rose to her feet. "My father wouldn't do something like that. His reputation means too much to him. He's worked too hard to throw everything away so stupidly."

Surely he would have mentioned something this big when she saw him at the hospital if he had.

"His much younger wife means more." Jensen's taunt told her everything she needed to know. "Why do you think a health nut like your father had a heart attack? The stress of knowing his past was closing in finally wore him down."

"Don't do this." Davida slowly sank back in her chair. "I have a boyfriend, and you have Lilly."

"Lilly finally gave up a few months back." Jensen laughed at her tenacity. Sadly, she'd been more interested in his status than in him. "She was cuddled up with some boy toy restaurateur ten years her junior two days after I refused her ultimatum. She didn't know I knew she'd been seeing him on the side for a good three months. As for your boyfriend, I don't think he means that much to you."

"Why would you say that?" Thomas was a good man. "You don't know anything about us."

"I know you." That was enough. "You would have requested a divorce a long time ago if you were serious." Davida winced at the accuracy of his statement. "You've been seeing the man for close to two years without getting much past a good-night kiss on the cheek. As far as you're concerned, we're still married, and we will be until the divorce goes through."

She was outraged he'd believe anything so foolish. Let him believe what he wanted. Nothing could be further from the truth. While they had yet to have sex for reasons that had nothing to do with him, it wasn't true they'd stopped at a few innocent kisses.

"I'd also say neither of you is all that serious, or you would be more than casual friends long before now. Face it, Davi. You're stuck on your wedding vows, and your beau gets off on dating powerful women."

While he was partially right, he was wrong about the most important part. They'd gone a good deal past a kiss on the cheek. Again, let him believe what he wanted.

"That sounds pathetic," Davida snapped. "Like we're biding time waiting for something better to come along."

"You are." Jensen gripped her hand. "But you're not pathetic. You're consumed by your work. You don't have time for a real relationship. That's why I'm giving you until the end of the season to wrap things up and come home."

There was a hint of desperation in his voice she'd never heard.

"Not going to happen." Davida shook her head. "We aren't reconciling, and I won't give up my dig. We have at least another ten seasons in the field. Probably longer. I'll need a couple of years after that to compile my notes and publish my findings.

That's non-negotiable. So sorry, but I'm booked for, oh, the next fifteen to twenty years."

"I'm not asking you to give up your work," Jensen informed her. "I'm asking you to renew our vows and give my father his grandson."

"Dan would make that requirement." Davida rolled her eyes. "As much as I love him, the man's a sexist pig."

"The man's a traditionalist," Jensen corrected. "While he's more than willing to give our daughters their own companies to run, Blake Enterprises has always passed from father to son. He's not about to change that now."

Even though the company vision had adapted with the times, Blake Enterprises had existed for four hundred years in one form or another. It was still going strong. With a seasoned history to back family tradition, his father saw no reason to fix what wasn't broken. The company wouldn't be worth billions if it were.

"I can't do this." Davida rose to her feet. "It's bad enough you're trying to blackmail me into motherhood, I find it unconscionable you expect me to pop out as many babies as it takes to get a boy. I'm not a brood mare, and I won't play your father's sick game."

"My father has nothing to do with you." Jensen twisted the truth to suit his purposes, knowing he would probably have to level with his wife before he was done. "As far as he's concerned, he doesn't care who I marry as long as he gets his grandson."

Davida made a rude noise, thinking that sounded more like Dan. The man wore charm like a second skin, but when it came to business, he was ruthless to the core.

"I feel differently." He would. "I don't see any point in marrying some woman I don't want when I already have the one I do."

Studying Davida through his father's eyes, Jensen accepted the truth of his words. While the miscarriage should be problematic, it wasn't. There were extenuating circumstances, so he'd take his chances. He didn't doubt for one minute they'd have the two or three little Blakes they always wanted.

"I won't do it." Davida reached for her jacket. "You're a jerk for asking."

"Then you can expect to find a couple of police officers camping outside your father's door by the time you get to the hospital." Jensen scrolled through his phone. "I have the Chief on auto-dial. All I have to do is make the call. He'll take care of the rest."

Davida cursed in her head. She should have expected something like this. Jensen was always a step or two ahead of the competition. Why should his personal life be any different? While he could have obtained a quickie divorce and married one of the women on his mother's wish list, her sudden appearance presented him with an opportunity too good to ignore.

"Fine. Give me a couple of hours." Davida opened the door. "I need to see my father. I'll give you a call when I finish. We can take it from there."

"Your two hours begin in fifteen minutes from now." That was about how long it would take her to reach her father's hospital room.

"After that, the talk is over."

Sitting back in his chair, Jensen watched his wife stomp from his office. As expected, the slammed door underscored what she thought of his actions. As much as he respected her fire, no one embezzled from his company and walked away free. Especially not his head accountant. While he might not go to jail, David would pay for his transgressions. He would make sure of that.

Putting his phone away, Jensen stared at two nearly full glasses of wine. While he contemplated drinking his, he poured both down the sink instead. The wine had lost its charm, even if it was a good year.

CHAPTER THREE

Resisting the urge to scream, Davida couldn't believe the mess she was in. Then again, she could. Her father was an idiot. He let Marti lead him around by the nose, and it had to stop. Like it or not, they had to live within their means. While her father's bank accounts would never touch Jensen's, he was well paid for his services. He always had been. More than enough to accommodate his bride in a style she had never been accustomed to.

Opening the car door, Davida gathered her thoughts. The last thing she wanted was to confront her father over his wrongdoing. But Jensen left her no choice. While a quarter mill was a drop in the bucket to her husband, he would never stand for his company being violated. Not when it sounded like her father was caught with his hand in the cookie jar.

That surprised her. She was confident David could have covered his tracks. But he hadn't. He probably thought he had time to return the money. Unfortunately, Jensen's father likely ordered one of those infamous surprise audits by an outside firm. One her father didn't see coming. Closing the car door much too hard, Davida cursed David's stupidity yet again.

Entering the hospital, she headed for her father's room and prayed he was alone. The last thing she needed was her step-mom losing it in front of her. The woman could be a simpering fool. Feeling guilty at the thought, Davi admitted Marti was neither stupid nor a fool. She was a talented special-needs teacher, and she respected her for that.

The woman was also falsely genteel, mildly selfish, and subtly manipulative about getting her way. She'd noticed that from the start. However, if her dad were happy, she wouldn't throw stones. He wasn't the easiest man to handle. She gave his wife kudos for effortlessly dealing with his antics.

Stopping in front of his room, she knocked softly before opening the door. Thankfully, Marti was nowhere to be seen. Walking over to drop a kiss on David's cheek, she was surprised he looked as good as he did. Much better than he had a couple of hours ago.

"I know you didn't expect to see me again until tomorrow." Davida pulled her chair close to the side of his bed. "But we need to talk."

"About what?" David picked at the covers on his bed. "I've already told you the attack was mild, and my heart is strong. It's going to take a few days to recover my strength."

Davida nodded as she digested his words. His story stayed the same, so she believed him.

"Where's Marti?" She didn't want the woman walking in on them. "I thought she would be here tonight."

"She dropped in while you were gone for a few minutes." Her father reached over to pat her hand. "She looked worse than I did, so I sent her home."

"She won't be back any time soon?" She hoped not. "I'm sorry I missed her."

"No, you're not." Her father dismissed her lie. "You were hoping she wouldn't be here to overhear this conversation."

"Why would you say that?" Davida hoped her father couldn't see through her. "You know I like Marti."

"You like her as much as you can like anyone as shallow as my wife." David's laugh was honest. "Sweetheart, you come by your personality honestly. Your mother was a brilliant woman and the love of my life, but she was a challenge." David hesitated briefly. "That isn't what I want at this stage of my life. While Marti's a mental lightweight compared to you or Luce, she loves me, and I love her. That's enough for now."

"Is it going to be enough when she learns what you've done?" The words popped out before she could stop them. "Or why you did it?"

"You've been talking to Jensen." David leaned back on his pillow and closed his eyes. "I was afraid of that. But whatever you think about Marti, she had nothing to do with this."

"You weren't trying to keep her happy?" Davida watched her father sit up straighter before turning to look at her. "You weren't buying things you couldn't afford?"

"No, I wasn't." David shook his head. "Marti has never asked for anything extravagant. She's content with what I give her, so don't try to pin my sins on her." He gave her more than she'd ever wanted. "I know her faults, Kiddo, but despite my wife's desire to have things her way, she isn't a bad person. Just young and foolish."

David laughed at the thought that anyone could have that kind of power over him, much less his sweet little Marti. She was a kid. A sexy, affectionate kid he adored, but still a child compared to him. Not even a decade older than Davi, she was nowhere near as worldly. Hardly the formidable opponent Luce had been. Snapping back to the matter at hand, he dreaded the words he had to say.

"The truth is I started gambling again." The confession took his daughter by surprise. "Not for long, and not often. But, with the kind of stakes we played for, it didn't take many losses to get into serious trouble."

"I can't believe you did that." Davida closed her eyes, expelling a heavy breath of horror. "That's the last thing I expected to hear." She thought those days were over. "In the kind of place no one talks about, with the kind of people who'd slit your throat for defaulting."

From the look on his face, she was right. "You almost got in trouble after Mom died. You would have if I hadn't snatched your butt out of the fire."

She'd threatened to tell Dan if he didn't get his act together back then. Fortunately, her promise worked. David stopped disappearing in the middle of the night, cold turkey, and became the father he needed to be. That was almost fifteen years ago. She thought that chapter of their lives was over. She was wrong. Looking at her dad's face, Davida shook her head, overwhelmed by her thoughts.

She wasn't quite fourteen when her mother died in a multicar pileup. Her father lost it soon after. He'd come unraveled before her eyes and started disappearing at all hours of the night. At first, she'd thought he was seeing someone on the sly, but that didn't make sense. David was still too lost in grief to look at another woman. If she hadn't worked up the courage to follow him, she wouldn't have known what he was doing.

But she had, and she was terrified by what she'd learned. Her father was burying his grief in the kind of backroom poker games that she shouldn't know existed. The kind that had men with guns and more booze flowing than a legitimate casino.

Fortunately, she'd taken her father's hand as he'd left that night and verbally knocked some sense into him before his vice got out of hand.

"I know." David closed his eyes. "I'm a fool, and I'm sorry. Between the stress of work and readjusting to married life, I needed an outlet to blow off steam."

"Dad, between you and me, jogging is an outlet." Davida's titter was slightly unhinged. "Stealing from Dan is professional suicide."

"I thought I could fix things before anyone knew." Famous last words. "Look, everything was good for a while. I didn't play that often, and I usually won.

Then Marti and I hit a rough patch. I was putting in a lot of overtime with that new merger, and Marti's father got sick. Between her work and helping Jim, she was gone too much.

We didn't see each other for days at a time, and when we did, we argued...While neither of us wanted a divorce, things were bad for a while...Bad...I started playing more and losing more. Not that much in the beginning. Nothing I couldn't pay back without Marti noticing."

He cast her a sheepish look.

"As the deficits grew, I kept thinking my luck would change. Before I knew it, I was in over my head." David hung his head in shame. "I had to pay up or get exposed. We both know Jensen would fire me if that happened. Like he's going to now."

Fire him or worse.

"I don't believe you." Davida rose from her seat to walk over to the window. "Instead of quitting when things went south, you bought into the lie, or did you give in to addiction?"

"I'm not addicted." David stared at his daughter's rigid back. "I gave it all up two years ago. I haven't been back since I made my last payment six months ago. I thought I would have everything cleared up before the discrepancies came to light. A couple of my investments were doing well, so I've put most of the money back already."

He could have put it all back if he'd sacrificed a chunk of his substantial savings, but he refused to do that. He wouldn't leave Marti financially deficient if anything happened to him. She didn't deserve that.

"This just keeps getting better and better." Davida turned from the window. "Exactly how much did you embezzle?"

"Embezzle is such an ugly word." David closed his eyes. "I borrowed close to two hundred thousand, maybe more."

Maybe over double that, but who was counting?

"You lost two hundred thousand gambling?" Davida plopped inelegantly intp her chair. "I want to say you deserve whatever you get. I won't. You're still my dad, and I love you."

"I love you, too, but we both know you may be loving me through a glass partition before everything is done." That reality was finally sinking in. "Jensen isn't a forgiving man. Not where business is concerned."

Neither was Dan, but he might not know his failings yet. She hoped he didn't, although he probably did. The man knew everything connected to the business, even if he'd handed the reins to Jensen years ago.

"No, he isn't," Davida agreed, checking her watch. "But he won't send you to jail. I'll make sure of that."

"I don't see how." From the little he knew, the couple hadn't communicated since she left until today. "You aren't together anymore."

"Jensen wants to be." Davida rolled her eyes at her father's incredulous expression. "You're right, and it's nothing like that. The truth is, Dan has Jensen in a bind, and Jensen has me in a bind thanks to you."

Staring at her dad, Davida briefly resented how intertwined her life had been with the Blakes for as long as she could remember. Her father started at the company in the accounting department straight out of college. By the time she came along, he had worked his way up to lower management. By the time she was in high school, he was their head accountant.

While no one ever expected her to marry the heir, she'd known Jensen in passing her whole life. However, they'd moved in different circles for a lot of reasons, including the fourteen-year age difference between them.

"What's that supposed to mean?" David's expression stayed calm. "It's not hard to believe Jensen wants you back. He was in a bad way the first year after you left. Eventually, he snapped out of it and fell into his old ways." Catching her eye, David told her what she needed to hear. "Let's just say he hasn't been a model husband the last four years."

More like in "flavor of the week" mode from what she'd seen. Right. While not literally that bad, Davida had noticed the revolving door of girlfriends in the society pages over the past few years. From what she remembered, her father's timetable sounded right.

"I know." Davida shook her head. "We get the gossip rags overseas." Considering Jensen's maternal grandparents were minor British aristocracy, he featured in quite a few of them. "I guess the upside is he never asked for a divorce."

"Why would he?" Her father's laugh was ugly. "As long as he still has that ring on his finger, his bed warmers know they'll never win the prize. It also deters them from trying to manufacture that unplanned pregnancy, although I doubt Jensen would fall for that old trick. He's much too in control of himself and the situation to ever father a child he didn't want."

"That's disgusting." Davida thought back over their earlier meeting, only to realize her father was right. Jensen was still wearing the wide gold band she'd placed on his finger seven long years ago. "But effective for the scum-sucking worm he's become."

"Honey, you can't blame him." Her father laughed at her outrage over being used like that. "He's a man magnet for every high-caliber gold digger he meets."

And his fair share of bottom feeders as well.

"I can blame him for a lot of things." Davida huffed. "But I blame you more."

Giving him a minute to digest her words, she whipped out her phone and dialed a number.

"Jensen, I don't care if I'm interrupting that emergency meeting you mentioned." She listened to whatever he was saying. "I need another hour to talk things over with my dad." Her tone brooked no argument. "I don't care if you have a dinner date in an hour. Call it off or be late. I won't be pressured into doing something I'll regret for the rest of my life." Rolling her eyes, Davida tapped her foot in anger. "Dad is a grown man. He made his bed. He can lie in it. As for you and Dan and your nasty little scheme, you can both step straight to hell for all I care. If you want my help, let me decide to offer it."

Nodding at what was being said on the other end, Davida ended the call and dropped the phone back in her purse. As weary as this made her, she had to finish what her father started. It wasn't the kind of thing you left hanging.

"What was that all about?" David hit the button to raise the head of his bed to a sitting position. "The bind I've put you in?"

"You'd better believe it." Davida snapped. "Jensen wants to reconcile so he can turn me into a baby factory. Dan has given him the ultimatum of marrying and producing a son in the next year or losing the company."

"That sounds like the wily old codger." David's laugh was long and deep. "Don't think for one minute the man doesn't know what he's doing."

"What's that supposed to mean?" Davida demanded. "You're not saying he knew Jensen would try to take the easy way out?"

"I'm saying he knew his son would try to reconcile with his wife." David shook his head. "It's no secret you're the only woman to tame the tiger. Cut the arrogant Blake heir down to size. Davi, whatever you think, Jensen never stopped loving you. He was devastated when he came home to find you gone."

"Yeah, well, he shouldn't have been carrying on with another woman." Davida snapped. "I'd still be there if he hadn't."

"Carrying on with another woman?" David repeated. "Surely you didn't believe he was cheating on you with Sharon Sloane?" Her father studied her defensive expression. "My God, you did."

He'd known she was devastated by how those pictures looked, but he never realized she believed they were true. He thought he'd convinced her that they weren't. That her husband wouldn't touch that amoral alley cat with a ten-foot pole. He was wrong.

"Maybe." Davida agreed. "I know better now. But there's more to the story than that."

"Then you'd better tell me before your time runs out." David motioned to her watch. "I know it's been close to twenty minutes since you called Jensen."

"I was seven weeks pregnant when that picture broke," Davida quietly told him. "I lost the baby that night."

"Why didn't you tell me?" Her father reached out for her. "You don't blame Jensen?"

"I did," Davida admitted. "Until I admitted I was just as much at fault. I was killing myself working on my dissertation. I never slept, and I barely ate. I was physically and mentally overwhelmed between school and Tara's charities. Honestly, I think the pictures were just the straw that broke the camel's back."

She didn't necessarily believe her high level of stress had directly caused her miscarriage, but it didn't help. The Sharon incident was the icing on the cake.

"Your mother was pregnant a couple of years before you," David told her. "We were ecstatic, and everything was fine until Luce lost that baby for no reason. That may not mean anything in your case, or it might mean everything."

Davida nodded, digesting his words.

"You were an accident we were glad to see happen, but your mom wasn't willing to try again after you. She was a wreck the whole time she was pregnant."

He thought she was foolish then; he felt the same now.

"I think it was just one of those things, and everything would have been fine." David patted her hand. "Luce was afraid, so I never pressured her to expand our family. She was too much like you. She wanted to be in the field every chance she had, so another child or two would have been a burden."

Davida knew he was right. She'd seen the pictures of her mom on digs with her playing somewhere in the background. She'd loved hanging out with Luce for as long as she could remember. Her Mom was a card, and her father tolerated her crazy antics. Her co-workers adored her, and she made the most amazing discoveries without even trying. Davida knew she was three or four when she'd decided she wanted to be just like her mom. She'd never looked back.

"You may be right." Davida smiled at her memories. "She was always leaving you at the office and dragging me off to some dig somewhere."

"Yes, she was." David agreed. "I guess I'm fortunate she loved American history so much that I never had to worry about her running off overseas. There were enough digs nearby that you were never any farther than a state or two over at any given time."

"Except the time you made her mad when I was twelve and she took off to Switzerland for six months without telling you." Her father had climbed on his high horse and forbade her mother from accepting a guest lecturer position at a college in Chicago for a semester. "I still don't know what you did to make her come home."

"Let's just say I went over there determined to convince her of what she was missing and leave it at that." Her father smiled at the memory. "You're almost out of time, so what's your decision?"

"I don't know," Davida admitted. "I don't love Jensen, and I don't believe he loves me even if you do." Her upraised hand halted his words. "It doesn't matter either way. What he needs me to do has nothing to do with love."

"It should." Her father reminded her somberly. "Creating life should have everything to do with love and nothing to do with duty."

Exactly why he didn't push Marti to start a second family. While he would love to, she didn't have a maternal bone in her body. She loved her job and her children, but at the end of the day, she didn't want little ones underfoot. She wanted to shower him with love, and he was content with that. Especially considering this recent turn of events. He didn't want to saddle her with young children if anything happened to him.

"It doesn't matter." Davida shook her head in resignation. "I'll do what I have to, but I'm doing it my way."

"You're not going to make it easy for him, are you?" He knew his daughter well. "Jensen won't make it easy on you either."

"No, he won't," Davida smirked. "However, he'll agree to my terms in the end, or he can find a new incubator. As for you, if you ever do anything this stupid again, I'll call the cops myself."

Davida's tone was steely. She would do exactly as she said, and her father knew it. His irresponsibility had caused this mess. His daughter wouldn't let him forget it. All things considered, it was just punishment.

"What about Thomas?" David mentioned the man she hadn't thought about. "How will he feel about your reconciliation?"

"Disappointed he lost his bragging rights," Davida stated dryly. "Other than that, no great loss. We enjoy each other's company. End of story."

Not quite, but she wasn't going there with her father. She was a grown woman living her life. He wasn't entitled to intimate details of that life any more than Jensen was.

"If you were anyone else, I'd be sorry you wasted two years of your life on a man you don't love." David shook his head. "But I know you. If you'd wanted anything more with Tom, you'd have it by now. Jensen is the only man to knock you off your stride, and he married you."

"I married him," Davida corrected. "And you see where that got me."

"What I see is the two of you finally handling a situation that should have been handled a long time ago," David told her quietly. "Don't waste the opportunity with bitterness over a mess neither of you created."

If she had to blame anyone, she needed to blame the shameless hussy who manufactured that photo in the first place. David firmly believed they'd still be together without Sharon's interference. He knew it. They challenged and complemented each other too well for life to be otherwise.

"Dad, I'm only doing this because I don't have a choice." Davida reminded him. "I don't know what's going to happen, and it scares me. All I can hope is this isn't a mistake that will destroy my life all over again."

"Do you want children?" David searched her face. "We've never really talked about that."

"I did," Davida admitted. "I wouldn't have married Jensen if I didn't. I can't see Dan and Tara not having grandkids. They're too family oriented."

While they held their offspring to high standards, both of her in-laws genuinely loved each other and their children. For a family steeped in tradition and expectations, they'd allowed each of their children to choose their paths. Even Jensen. He was never forced to follow in his father's footsteps. He'd wanted to. He'd worked hard to earn the right to head the company he loved so well. She couldn't take that away from him, and she wouldn't try.

"Then you're right." David rubbed her hand. "You are going to complicate your life, but you certainly won't destroy it. No matter what happens, you'll never regret that child."

She would love her child—or children— with all her heart as her mother had. That wasn't in question. They both knew that.

"I hope you're right." Davida glanced at her watch. "Right now, all I care about is Jensen not having you arrested." She leaned over to kiss his forehead. "But, if you don't walk that narrow line from now until the day you die, I'll do it for him."

"You won't have to," David reassured her. "I'm going to pay every dime back. While I'm not sure how I'll do that once Jensen fires me, I'll have plenty of time to figure it out."

"Yes, you will." Davida opened the door. "I'll give you a call as soon as I finish with my husband." The word rolled off her tongue with a touch of acid. "If it's too late, I'll call you in the morning."

"Sounds good." David watched her walk through the doorway. "I'll tell Marti you said hello."

Davida closed the door behind her, thinking she would do that herself tomorrow. Eventually, she'd let her father know his job was safe and his debt was paid. She couldn't do that yet. For one thing, she didn't know her ploy would work. For another, he needed to stew in his juices for a while. He'd appreciate her sacrifice more when he did.

CHAPTER FOUR

E xiting the elevator, Davida walked down the hall, determined to open the door before Jensen could. She felt de-
moralized when he ushered her into his office before she could
knock. Like a naughty student summoned to the principal's office. Moving as quietly as possible, she opened the door and
stepped inside.

Jensen was seated behind his desk, casually studying a file
as though he'd known she was there all along. That shouldn't
surprise her. Not really. She'd called to let him know she was
on her way. He'd then let her know she shouldn't dawdle. He'd
cancelled his date and ordered her favorite takeout from the
neighborhood dive. It would be there by the time she was,
which was fine by her. She didn't know she was hungry until he
mentioned food.

"Soup's on." Jensen set the file aside. "I ordered your usual."

"By usual, I hope you mean the fried shrimp and clam
box with a soda?" She hadn't eaten anything like this in years.
"Goody."

Fish and chips at the Trousered Viking didn't count. No
way. While delicious and quintessentially British, nothing beat
Joe's Place when it came to greasy spoon.

"Good." Jensen walked around his desk. "Then we eat first
and talk later."

"Works for me." Sitting in a leather chair, Davida opened
her box and laughed at the double containers of tartar and
cocktail sauces she always requested. With any luck, Jensen

would toss her his extra ketchup packets like he used to as well. "It smells delicious."

"Because it is." Jensen agreed. "I don't think I've ordered this since you left." He passed her a fried oyster from his seafood platter. "It reminded me too much of the early days."

"What do you mean?" Davida paused hush puppy in hand. "All those times I dropped by the office after hours when we ordered takeout?"

Back in the day, she didn't want anyone to know she was dating the boss. Especially her father. Considering the place was mostly deserted by six, their secret was safe enough. The guys manning the front desk and walking the halls knew better than to gossip. Besides, for all they knew, they were just friends. She wasn't the boss's usual style. Too young and more class than flash.

"Something like that." Jensen agreed. "I've missed those days."

"Don't try to butter me up." She wouldn't admit she'd missed them as well. "Let's just enjoy our food and talk business later."

"We can do that." Jensen turned back to his dinner, deciding to keep things neutral until Davi was ready to talk. "How was your father?"

"Doing better than expected." She answered honestly. "He looked rough earlier, but he looks okay now. He'll probably go home in a day or two."

"How's Marti?" It was still hard to believe his head accountant had married the woman. It was even harder to believe they'd stayed together. No one believed it would last. "As perfectly pulled together as always?"

"I don't know." Davida sat back in her chair. "I haven't seen her. Dad sent her home to rest."

"He probably needed to escape her constant, mindless chatter," Jensen said what she wouldn't. "That's the main reason I'm not fond of your stepmother."

"She's not all bad." Davida wouldn't admit she felt the same. "She's a nice person, and she makes Dad happy. That's all that matters."

"It doesn't hurt that she's a head turner, twenty years younger than him." Jensen laughed softly. "Admit it, that's half the charm."

"I think we're both wrong." Davida set her empty box aside. "I think my dad loves her because she loves him. Mom was like me. Not the easiest thing to live with. Marti's softer and more feminine. She dotes on him in ways Mom never did."

"And your father eats it up." Dropping both empty boxes in the can, Jensen rose to his feet. "Let me answer the phone and we'll get down to business."

Ignoring the conversation droning in the background, Davida gathered her thoughts. She wasn't sure how she felt about any of this. What she did know was that she needed to buy time to come to terms with the whole mess without throwing her father to the wolves.

"I'm done." Jensen's voice dragged Davida from her thoughts. "I know you've spent the past few hours weighing the pros and cons. Let's hear what you decided. I'm willing to hear anything once."

Davida rolled her eyes.

"Fine, you don't prosecute, and my father keeps his job." Davida blurted the first thing on the tip of her tongue. "Do a few surprise audits throughout the year. Give him a chance to redeem himself. I don't think you have anything to worry about in the future."

"Neither do I." Jensen agreed. "If he steps out of line again, I will prosecute. No questions asked. No mercy."

"I'll help you." Davida laughed at the look he shot her. "I also need three to four months to wrap up my work on site. I'll finish my notes and field reports when I return stateside. Leslie may have to take over for a few weeks next season if I do conceive, but I expect to be back in the field as soon as possible after the baby is born."

"If you still feel that way when the time comes, we'll talk." Jensen conceded, knowing he'd entertain that fight when he had to. "I'll give you the time you need to wrap up this season, but we can't waste any time after that." Davida knew what he was saying without him saying it. "From what you've said, we may need extra time."

Resisting the urge to respond that they didn't know that Davida bit her tongue. She wanted to suggest IVF, but Jensen wouldn't go for it. As much as she didn't want to engage in meaningless sex, she didn't want to go the impersonal route either. Her child shouldn't know their parents were off from the start. The situation was twisted enough without adding smoke and mirrors to the mix.

"Fine." Davida snapped. "While I understand your sense of urgency, I need time to wrap my mind around this situation." She rolled her eyes at his slightly offended expression. "Look, I've spent the past five years expecting divorce papers any day. It's not like we were trying to work out our differences."

Jensen flashed the universal "whose fault is that?" look she wholly despised.

"There's also the fact that, while I wasn't intimately involved with anyone, you've made up for both of us."

He didn't need to know that it was largely because she hadn't run into anyone who caught her fancy. Not until she'd met Tom. Not enough to further complicate already complicated work environments anyway. That she and Tom had yet to consummate their relationship had more to do with factors beyond their control than reluctance on either side.

"I guess I have." Jensen agreed. "They didn't mean anything."

"I'm sure they'd love to know that." Davida huffed. "It didn't look that way in the pictures."

"You know things aren't always how they look." He refused to mention Sharon's name. "Davida, you were around long enough to know the game. Those women used me as much as I used them. Everyone knew the score from the start."

"That's cold, even for you." She'd witnessed that ruthless streak in business, never in their personal lives. "Surely someone in there was more than a pretty face."

"Not a one," Jensen admitted. "I made it clear from the start that divorce wasn't an option. I kept my place, and they kept theirs. It was what it was, end of story. Any woman accepting my offer wanted social or financial advancement more than they wanted me. We both got what we wanted in the end."

"You're lucky you didn't get more than you bargained for." Davida gently reminded him. "One of those women could have turned up pregnant."

"Not by me." Jensen sat back in his chair. "The one time I was careless cost me everything."

She ignored the pain flickering briefly through his eyes. It wasn't something she was willing to contemplate. Not yet anyway.

"The two times." Jensen reluctantly confessed. "I was careless to trust Sharon."

Davida bit her tongue to keep from verbally agreeing with him. The woman was a vicious viper wrapped in pretty packaging. Neither of them had known the extent of her evil ways at the time. She'd taken his word for it and believed they were over and done.

"But I didn't have any reason not to." Davida snorted at that one. "She left me, not the other way around. If anyone held a grudge, it should have been me."

Right. Sharon didn't feel the same. Her future actions proved it. From what she'd heard at the time, Jensen returned to the dating scene insultingly fast after the demise of his engagement. He was neither heartbroken nor humiliated. More like grateful not to have that noose around his neck, and he'd shown it.

It didn't matter that no one ever believed the happy couple was in love. In lust? Maybe. In love? Never. They were uniting two powerful dynasties in a time-honored manner. Nothing more and nothing less. Jensen's parents had done the same. Fortunately, somewhere along the way, they fell deeply in love.

He knew that would never happen for him. His fiancée was much too narcissistic to cultivate a meaningful relationship. She didn't care about family. She cared about attaining her desires. If children were a necessary evil on the road to success, she'd pop out a couple for a nanny to raise. Sharon had never hidden her true feelings from anyone. With hindsight, he realized the woman shared none of his values, even if she ticked his parents' imaginary boxes.

However, he'd found her tolerable, and he'd appreciated the sparks between them. He'd thought Sharon felt the same. He'd been prepared to take the next step and surrender his freedom to Blake Enterprises. However, his lover had other ideas. She'd suddenly returned his ring on their quick getaway to the French Riviera mere weeks before the wedding.

Once he'd gotten over the shock, he'd dreaded telling his parents their marriage was off until he'd detected that gleam of relief in his father's eyes. Dan wasn't fond of Sharon either. Tara had been less understanding. Considering his fiancée's mother was one of her closest friends, she'd demanded to know what he'd done wrong. He didn't have an answer. Nothing except that Sharon hooked a bigger fish when he wasn't looking.

"Then again, I forgot she wanted to reconcile when her new relationship petered out."

Davida couldn't believe he'd never told her that. Then again, she could. Another piece of the puzzle fell into place. While Jensen wasn't a vengeful person, Sharon was. She saw an opportunity to kill two birds with one stone, so she took it.

Not only had her ploy seized the media's imagination, but she'd sown discord in their marriage. She'd done more than that. She'd destroyed their union in one fell swoop.

"I turned her down flat. Dumping me three weeks before the wedding forfeited her right to a do-over." Jensen continued. "It didn't hurt I'd run into you by then, and you weren't the snot-nosed brat I remembered anymore."

She was a striking tomboy with a casual, youthful confidence he'd found captivating. One who easily morphed into a curvy, breathtaking woman with the intelligence to match when she needed to. Add a sharp tongue and the wit to match her stubborn willingness to take him on, and he was done. He'd proposed on their six-month anniversary and married her before the year was out.

Giving Davida the once-over, Jensen was mildly surprised he never once regretted giving up his freedom. Not as he would have with Sharon. Not even after their breakup. They'd spent two tumultuously happy years together before unprovoked nastiness opened the gates of hell.

He still remembered that night like it was yesterday. He'd returned from a business trip to discover their home void of his wife and that disgusting article resting innocently on their kitchen counter. In the blink of an eye, everything he knew and loved was gone. He hadn't known what had happened. Not until he'd read the magazine his wife left behind.

It was clear that Davida drew her conclusions from what she saw. If only he'd known it was so much worse, he might have turned things around long before now. He could have forced her to hear his side of the story at worst. Proven he wasn't guilty at the best. But he didn't know anything. Not until a few hours ago.

As things were, they had never spoken after that night. Not until today. Not in person anyway. They'd communicated through lawyers on the rare occasions they had anything to say. That was it. Fortunately, her father had created the opportunity he needed to reach her again.

"I guess I wasn't." She was very much still that snot-nosed kid: he just didn't know it. "I was getting ready to start that summer semester in the UK, and I'd dropped by the office to tell my dad goodbye on the way to the airport."

Shockingly, Jensen had fallen hard based on that one brief meeting in a way that surprised everyone. Davi was nothing he was usually attracted to. She was too studious, too naive, too young, and most importantly, in some circles, too lacking in social connections. However, despite the strikes against her, she *was* the one he wanted. At any cost.

"You wouldn't even let him come in an hour late to see me off that day. Some nonsense about his needing to entertain some client who'd flown in from Japan unexpectedly."

Davida shot him a dirty look reminiscent of the one she'd given that day.

"You let me have it for that one, too." She'd been twenty if she were a day. "I'll never forget how cute you were with steam coming out of both your ears."

"I wasn't cute, and my father was humiliated when you told him what I'd done," Davida admitted. "He wasn't happy I'd been rude to his boss's son. If he'd known you followed me to London a few months later, he would have egged me on. He's always thought you were too old for his little girl."

"So says the man who robbed the cradle." Jensen's husky laugh betrayed just how comfortable he was back in her presence. "I had business in London. Showing up at your flat that night was an easy side trip."

"I didn't know that." Davida reached up to pull the clip from her hair before shaking her locks free. "Way to burst my bubble. I thought you'd flown all that way just for me."

"No, you didn't." Jensen rested his feet on top of his desk, imagining Dan's frown at seeing him looking so undignified. "You would have thought I was a stupid git trying to get in your pants if you had."

"You're right." Davida rubbed her temple in that unconscious way that betrayed that she was holding a headache at bay. "My dad let slip you were going to London and Edinburgh on business before I left. I was flattered you made time to see me between appointments. I think that was the night I started falling for you."

"I was already done." Jensen leaned back in his chair. "And I wasn't happy about it. You were way too young for me."

"I was almost twenty-one going on thirty." And a total babe in the woods when it came to romance. "My mom was one of the best archaeologists in her field. I was determined to follow in her footsteps. You already know I took college courses while I was in high school and finished my B.A. ahead of the curve at the top of my class. Surely you didn't think I'd let a spoiled rich boy intimidate me?"

"You didn't." Jensen agreed. "I think I was intimidated."

"Hardly," Davida snarked. "You took me to that pub the first night and got me drunk."

"I took you to that pub and let you do what you wanted." He corrected. "How was I supposed to know you didn't drink?" It had taken all of a glass of wine before he'd put the skids on. "You probably still don't." Not much and not often, anyway. "Besides, you weren't exactly drunk. More like amusingly tipsy."

"Whatever." Davida walked over to his mini fridge for a bottle of water. "Dad would have kicked your butt for getting me amusingly tipsy."

"Probably." Jensen agreed. "But what matters is I didn't take advantage of you when I probably could have."

He could have, and the thought crossed his mind. Fortunately, the voice of reason reminded him that he was playing for keeps. Moving too fast would cost him everything, so he didn't.

"No, you didn't." Not until he had that engagement ring on her finger. "You were a gentleman. You always have been."

"I always will be." Jensen reached across his desk to swipe her water bottle. "Whatever you think, I care about you." Twisting the lid, he handed it back to her. "I always did."

"Yeah, well, I cared about you, too." Davida took a sip of water. "Unfortunately, there have been five years to stop caring about each other."

"I guess there have been." Jensen closed his eyes for a moment, mildly surprised at the sharp pain her words elicited. "Why are you entertaining reconciliation if you feel that way?"

"Why do you think?" Davida stared into his eyes. "Do you seriously think I'd let my father go to jail over this?"

Again, he was surprised that every word felt like a physical blow.

"Is that the only reason?" Jensen leaned forward. "To keep David out of jail."

"Pretty much," Davida answered honestly. "I'm sorry if you were hoping for a different response."

He had been.

"I tried to find you all those years ago," Jensen admitted. "I did." He leaned back in his chair and crossed his arms. "Your father refused to give me any information, no matter how I bribed or threatened."

CHAPTER FIVE

Davida laughed softly at the frustration in his voice.

"My father didn't refuse anything." She decided to put him out of his misery. "Dad didn't have anything to give. All my emails come through the same professional email address I've used all over Europe." The one she'd set up on the steppes. "The only telephone number he had was a cell he knew I'd change the minute you called me. Anything I've mailed him recently was sent from London when I drove down from the dig. I've never sent him anything about Deira, and I'm not mentioned by name in any of the local articles about our discoveries. All Dad has ever known is that I'm the lead archaeologist on a site somewhere in England, and I'm happy. He's never pushed for more."

David wasn't good at keeping secrets at the best of times. In this instance, he might have deliberately sabotaged her for the greater good. She never gave him that opportunity. He'd known changing that number and never calling again was a promise, not an empty threat. Fortunately, his only child meant more than his job ever did.

"I see." He steepled his fingers. "You didn't want me to find you, did you?" Jensen decided that greasy spoon may not have been the best choice for dinner. "You wouldn't have covered your tracks so well if you had."

"No, I didn't." Davida took a healthy swig of water as she chose her words carefully. "Under the circumstances, I don't think you would act any differently." While his look indicated otherwise, she doubted it. "That picture was damning, and that kiss was more than a peck on the lips."

There was no denying where Sharon's hand was if he'd tried to.

"I didn't molest Sharon." Jensen resisted the urge to call the woman what she was. "She molested me. While I don't know how she discovered I was at the club, my meeting wasn't a secret. Anyone could have given her my itinerary."

"It wouldn't be hard to bribe someone at your hotel to learn where you were." Not only that, but it was well known in the business community that he and his colleagues would usually unwind over dinner and drinks after a meeting. Usually at the club. "I'm assuming you invited Sharon to join you when she suddenly appeared."

"There wasn't any reason not to." Jensen agreed. "Our fathers are business associates, and our mothers are dear friends."

Davida knew that. Family connections meant Sharon had lurked on the periphery of their lives from the start. She'd never been a threat. Not to her. A casual drink at a social club was fine. What the other woman did wasn't. While she doubted it would have made much difference at the time, a part of her wished she'd known the truth five years ago.

As for Jensen, he'd issued the invitation expecting to spend a cordial few minutes catching up on Sharon's exploits since their engagement ended. He'd been clueless about her true intent. Her behavior hadn't betrayed anything. She'd sat in the chair beside him and ordered her usual glass of Pinot Grigio while he'd stuck with the Single Malt he'd nursed all evening. He'd thought the story ended when he'd rebuffed her blatant pass.

His first inkling that something underhanded had occurred was when he returned home to a deserted house. It appeared that the magazine had timed the release of those photos just right to ensure Davida saw them before he even knew they existed. While he hadn't necessarily realized it at the time, today he was confident that bit was Sharon's handiwork. She'd wanted revenge, and she got it. While the pass wasn't unexpected, the hidden photographer with the long-range lens was. In the end, his ex-fiancée's plan was as effective as it was diabolical.

Jensen snorted at the thought that if anyone should have wanted vengeance, it was him. Sharon had walked out on their wedding three weeks before the ceremony. Her actions cost her parents a small fortune in deposits, and him the earnest money on that swanky townhouse she had to have. The only upside was that he'd been able to return the ring.

"It doesn't matter anymore." Davida's voice was quiet. "What does matter is that I have years of resentment to work through. While I forgave you for what happened a lifetime ago, I don't think I can forget it. I'm not sure I can do this even if I wanted to."

Jensen bit his tongue. Whether she was willing to admit it or not, she didn't have a choice. Between him losing the company or her father going to jail, David was expendable. While there were any number of women he could marry, he'd rather tangle with the devil he knew than one he didn't. His only attempt at matrimony hadn't left a pleasant taste in his mouth.

"You won't know unless you try." Jensen kept his tone even and reasonable. "From what I remember, neither of us had a problem doing what it takes to procreate."

"So, we were great in bed." That wasn't up for debate. "Sex has nothing to do with being good, loving parents or providing a stable home environment for a child. Any kid we bring into the world deserves that much."

"I hope you don't think I won't love our child regardless of what happens between us." Jensen wanted to shake some sense into the woman sitting across from him. "Or provide a stable home. You know me better than that."

"I'm sorry." Davida worried her bottom lip. "I do." His declaration wasn't what bothered her. "Look, the bottom line is I'm not sure I can get past your other women."

Ignoring his stunned look, Davida forged ahead. "I know we were legally separated, and we were living apart." Far apart. "I'm not even saying you didn't have the right to move on. You did. I honestly never thought I cared. But, faced with the prospect of reconciling, I do."

He'd betrayed her many times over. They both knew it.

"I see." He should have seen this coming. "Somehow, that doesn't surprise me."

He'd always known fidelity was important to Davida. Infidelity was probably the only thing that could destroy their marriage, and it had. However, even knowing that, he'd moved on with his life. He had to. His family, his business, and his position demanded it.

"It surprises me," Davida admitted. "Since you were out of sight and out of mind, it wasn't that hard to ignore the occasional photograph featuring you and the flavor of the week."

While not exactly true, it wasn't a complete lie either. She'd ignored the photographs as much as possible. But they still hurt. Until she'd convinced herself they didn't. Fortunately, there was an upside to the pain. The females changed frequently, so she knew the liaisons were more hook-ups than serious. Some perverse part of her was pleased by that.

"Davi, I won't give you an insincere apology," Jensen toyed with his pen. "And I won't lie. You left without a word. I was hurt and angry that first year." His universe had imploded without warning. How else could he feel? "When I snapped out of it, I buried my emotions in meaningless flings."

He refused to dignify those casual encounters by calling them what they weren't. Speaking plainly, they were hook-ups, nothing more or less. They weren't relationships or affairs. That would require a depth of commitment he never felt. Nor, despite any protests to the contrary, did his intimate partners feel different. However, he was a big fish in a big pond and quite the catch if they caught him. Well, he was already caught seven years ago, and he didn't see that changing. Not if he played his cards right.

"While your lawyer never told me what happened, I knew it was serious. Out of respect for you, I signed the separation papers and left it at that. I didn't want to cause you more pain, but I didn't want a divorce. I still don't."

He'd decided not long after his first wedding fell through that when he finally tied the knot, he was committed for life. Committed and faithful. He wanted what his parents had, or he wouldn't do it. His stance hadn't changed in the years since. He was married, and he intended to stay that way. Despite Davida's reservations, he wouldn't let go. Not until he had to cut his losses and walk away. He hoped that day would never come.

"Jensen, I need to level with you." Davida leaned forward in her seat. "I don't want this to work."

She was surprised by the venom in her voice.

"You think I don't see that?" Jensen leaned forward in his seat as well. "My father's not a fool, and he hasn't lost his mind. Your father played into his hands a long time ago. Dan probably knew what David was doing almost from the start. I wouldn't put it past him to have waited for the perfect opportunity to spring this trap on all of us."

Jensen hadn't meant to reveal that truth unless he had to. He played his cards close to his chest. Shared knowledge as knowledge was needed. Not one second before. However, Davida rarely allowed him to play by his own rules. She always kept him on his toes.

"What do you mean?" Davida's tone was wary. "This has nothing to do with business and everything to do with getting us back together?"

"Something like that," Jensen admitted. "Dan loves you like a daughter, and he knows we're good together."

He refused to contemplate how good they were in every respect.

"Davi, he's old school. He doesn't approve of my dating habits. He doesn't approve of you leaving me. He doesn't approve of divorce. He believes our marriage can work if we put our differences aside, so he's forcing the issue as only he can."

"Right." Davida rolled her eyes. "Your Dad was always unrealistic where family was concerned."

"Not that unrealistic," Jensen corrected. "He sees things other people miss, and I think he may be right." He reached across the desk to clasp her hand. "Even if I thought he was wrong, I'd still want to try for his sake."

Releasing her hand, he rose to his feet and walked over to stand in front of the picture window behind his desk. Dragging his hand through his hair, he contemplated how much he should share. Both what he was willing to share and what he had a right to share.

However, staying tight-lipped could cost him everything. Davida stuck to her guns on a good day. Today was far from good. Right now, she was exhausted, confused, and angry. She could easily decide to catch the next flight back to England and leave her father twisting in the wind.

He wouldn't put that past her unless he could change her mind. Give her a viable reason to give them that second chance he wanted. No, needed, and not just professionally speaking. Seeing Davida had reawakened all the feelings he'd tried to bury. Both the lovingly sweet and the explicitly erotic. There was just something about the woman that ticked all his boxes both mentally and physically, and he wouldn't change a thing. Taking a deep breath, he made up his mind and settled back in his chair.

"Dan doesn't think anyone knows." Jensen kept his tone even. "But his doctor called me a few weeks back." He weighed his words carefully. "Dad has a slow-growing blood cancer that could turn acute any time. The name isn't important. The fact that he has six months to a year left, if he's lucky, is. He could die next week if he isn't."

From the look in his eyes, Jensen wasn't lying. While they might butt heads occasionally, he adored his parents. The impending loss of his father and best friend was devastating.

"Crap." Davida wasn't sure how she felt about that. "How did everything get so complicated so fast?"

Forty-eight hours ago, she was up to her elbows in a game-changing skeleton and fabulously rich grave goods. Now, she was in the middle of more emotional crises than she'd seen in years. Life wasn't fair, and she hated drama. Especially the family kind.

"How do you think? We walked when we should have talked." Jensen responded honestly. "We swept the nasty under the rug and pretended it would go away if we ignored it long enough."

Nasty that he suspected would bite him on the butt before the night was over. He had yet to process that he'd lost a child he never knew he'd fathered. When that hit, he didn't want Davida anywhere near him. God only knew how he would handle it. He didn't.

He'd probably take the edge off the emotional pain by nursing several fingers of expensive Scotch whisky and going to bed. Alone. However, he wouldn't get inebriated. He hadn't done that since his college days, and he wouldn't start now. He didn't know what he would say to Davi if his inhibitions were lowered, but he doubted it would be anything good. It was better to keep his wits about him in her presence.

Right now, he was finding it hard to believe the woman he still loved hated him for years without just cause. Without ever bothering to hear his side of the story. That wasn't like her. Not the Davida he knew. The whole situation was insane. The woman was always fair and reasonable. Until she suddenly wasn't. Blaming pregnancy hormones didn't excuse her actions.

Studying his wife, Jensen knew righteous indignation would crawl out of the woodwork eventually. When it did, he'd have a lot to work through. However, he couldn't afford to entertain that emotion anytime soon. He'd blow any chance at reconciliation if he did. Davida wouldn't take kindly to his outrage. Even if it was justified. She had yet to work through her issues. He knew her well enough to see the cracks in that tough façade.

"You may be right." Flashing him a confused look, she buried her face in her hands for a couple of minutes. "If my dad isn't blackmail enough, Dan's the final nail in the coffin. I might not like any of you very much right now, but I love that man. I'll give it a try for his sake. But if, and only if, you give me time to come to terms with doing what I swore I'd never do."

Reconciling never crossed her mind. Not even after she'd stopped blaming Jensen. That ship had sailed, and the door closed years ago. She'd moved on with her life in very real ways, even if Jensen hadn't.

"I can do that." Within reason. "What else is on your mind?"

"You can't interfere with writing and publishing my field notes." Davida continued. "I don't care what's happening with Blake Enterprises; my work comes first. People are depending on me sharing my work, so that's non-negotiable."

"Again, I can do that." To a point. "However, I'll expect you by my side for important business functions. That isn't negotiable either."

No matter where she was with her field notes. Or what continent she was on, for that matter. Appearances mattered in his world. When they reconciled, they'd have to present a united front. To appear divided could be disastrous both professionally and privately.

"I can do that."

Smirking unpleasantly, Davida decided an expensive shopping spree on Jensen's dollar was in order before she settled in to pursue her life's work. She'd traded in her stylish wife-of-the-future CEO wardrobe for the casual, comfortable attire more appropriate to her profession a long time ago.

"Oh, and dad isn't paying the last of what he owes." That was another deal breaker. "Dan forked over more than that for our wedding. He can eat the loss."

Her father couldn't have footed the bill for her high-society wedding if he'd wanted to. Then again, things wouldn't have been nearly as extravagant if she'd had the wedding of her dreams. As it was, she'd had the wedding befitting the next CEO of Blake Enterprises instead.

A part of her still resented being forced to endure that dog and pony show when all she'd wanted was a small, intimate ceremony surrounded by family and close friends. It was what they'd both wanted. Tara wouldn't hear of it. Their nuptials had to be one of the top ten society events of the year. Besides, there were associates on both sides of the pond that they couldn't afford to slight without seriously damaging the business.

Despite Jensen's willingness to buck his parents, she'd caved instead. For the business. Right. Not hardly. She'd known she couldn't afford to start on the wrong foot with her formidable mother-in-law when she had finally earned her reluctant acceptance. Her life would be hell if she did.

"I'm not sure Dan will see it that way, but I'll be sure to mention it when I give him your terms."

Looking at her husband, Davida knew he was more amused than chagrined by her shenanigans.

"It'll be okay. I know David's returned a healthy chunk of the money. He didn't cover his tracks as well as he thought there either. I'll take that as a good faith gesture that he's back on the straight and narrow."

Davida nodded. He'd better be.

"I also expect to dictate when and where we reconcile." Davida made her last demand. "I'm not willing to hop into bed like we haven't spent the past five years apart."

She couldn't if she wanted to. As unreasonable as she knew she was being, she couldn't help her feelings. Right now, just the thought of sex with Jensen made her want to hurl.

"I don't expect you to." Jensen watched her shift uncomfortably in her chair. "If things had gone my way, I would have found you years ago and straightened everything out from the start." Before he'd strayed. "As it was, I got the message you didn't want to be found and gave up the hunt."

He'd then drunk himself into a stupor for a few weeks before he'd finally snapped out of it and thrown himself into work. A few months later, he'd reentered the late-night party circuit. He hadn't looked back since. Or he hadn't until he got wind that his runaway bride was back in town. Thank goodness for nosy busybodies. Without the unsolicited help of a hospital volunteer, she would have slipped in and out of town with no one the wiser. Once he'd learned their breakup was more than a misunderstanding, he knew he'd made a big mistake. One that would take time to undo.

"Dan has us between a rock and a hard place with one way out." Jensen opened a desk drawer to remove a set of keys. "I suggest we fall in line and give him that grandson as soon as possible."

Looking up, he settled comfortably in his chair, looking far more cavalier than he felt.

"If you still want out after he's gone, I'll sign the divorce papers." He watched Davida mull over every word. "In the meantime, I'm not going to interfere with your work. However, I am going to demand that we both sincerely try to make this work. We owe our child that much."

"If we can even have a child." That fear still tickled around the edges of her consciousness. "What if we can't?"

'What if I can't?' she meant, and they both knew it.

"We hire that surrogate." He made it sound so simple. "He'll still be ours whether you carry him or not."

"Fine." Davida accepted his words, not sure she wanted to go that route. "Then you tentatively have a deal."

Very tentative by her demeanor.

"I thought you'd see it my way." Jensen looked smugly triumphant. "But you university types have to make things difficult with all that logic."

"Yeah, well, if we don't, business types will exploit every loophole we miss." Rising to her feet, Davida reached for her jacket. "As nice as some of this was, I need to leave. It's been a long day, and I'm fried."

"I'll walk you down." Jensen followed her across the room. "It's not that safe out there anymore."

"Not like the old days, huh?" When she used to come drag him home after midnight on those nights he worked too hard. "Somehow, that doesn't surprise me. This town has changed a lot since I left."

Watching him close and lock the door behind them, Davida didn't resist when he reached out to clasp her hand. She might as well start getting used to Jensen's touch now. He'd be doing a lot more than holding her hand before too long.

"I'm sorry you had to cancel your date." Davida offered. "I thought it was better we do this before I lost my nerve."

Jensen was glad she admitted that, since he felt the same.

"It wasn't a legitimate date." He smirked. "It was all business. I'm sure Jeanie would rather be home with her devoted husband than thrashing out contracts with her boss."

"Jeanie Hensley?" Not the brilliant young international law attorney Jensen hired on her recommendation. The one he'd promoted to his personal attorney within the year. "She's still here?"

"Not just here." Jensen squeezed her hand. "She's an invaluable asset and the head of her division. She married Ohira in Investment Law after you left."

"It took them four years to get together?" Davida couldn't believe what she was hearing. "Those two were making eyes at each other almost from the start."

"They were secretly living together almost from the start." Jensen laughed at all the sneaking around he'd known they were doing. While the company didn't have a hard rule against dating fellow employees, the unspoken understanding was there. Business stayed neater that way. "They came clean a few months after you left and got married three years ago."

"I bet they're a cute couple." Davida unlocked her car door. "Jeanie's cute anyway. I barely remember Ohira."

"Neither of them is cute." Jensen shook his head. "Talented, not cute. Let me refresh your memory. Jeanie's a six-foot-two skinny giraffe with a slight overbite, while Ohira's a stocky five-eight waddling penguin. He's put on twenty pounds since they married. Looks aside, they're both brilliant, well-liked employees I pay very well for their services."

"Then act like it." Davida couldn't help thinking Jensen was right.

Jeanie's fun, outgoing personality made her seem much cuter than she was. From what little she could remember about Akihiko Ohira, he used to be skinny, too. If he'd filled out some, marriage agreed with him. She'd have to look them up when she settled in.

"I'll give you a call sometime tomorrow after I wake up, and we can go from there." Davida turned back to her husband. "I need to see Dad in the morning and check in with the dig. You should probably know I have to be back in England by the end of the week. There are complications with a recent discovery that only I can deal with. I can't change that."

Her appointments were set long before her father's illness. They were written in stone, and they wouldn't wait.

"We'll talk tomorrow." Jensen dropped a light kiss on her lips as he pressed a key against her palm. "You should probably know I still have the house, and it's just as you left it. You should also know I've never taken anyone there but you."

Nodding, Davida silently acknowledged she'd read between the lines. She believed him. Jensen had never violated the sanctity of their home. Neither literally nor figuratively, speaking. There were some things even he wouldn't do. But he was still a skunk. However, knowing that went a long way towards reassuring her that there might be hope for them. Even if she didn't fully believe it yet. Closing her car door, she pulled out of the parking space, watching Jensen watch her through her rearview mirror.

CHAPTER SIX

Putting her phone on vibrate, Davida tucked it into her pocket before entering the hospital yet again. Considering the time, she had every idea Marti was seated by her father's bed. That would greatly limit their conversation when so many things needed to be said.

While she'd hoped to get here much earlier, it wasn't possible. She'd neglected her work far too long. It had to stop. As a result, she'd spent most of the morning talking with Leslie and dealing with minor hiccups popping up in her absence. Fortunately, an appointment had been rescheduled, and nothing needed her immediate attention. She could take an extra day or two to sort her issues on this side of the pond before she had to manage issues on the other. She wasn't sure if that was a blessing or a curse.

"Hello, Marti." Davida greeted the petite brunette with all the enthusiasm she could muster. "It's been a while."

"Yes, it has." Returning her stepmother's warm hug, Davida leaned over to drop a kiss on her father's head.

"Too long. I'd forgotten what it's like to be home."

"Now that you're here, I'm going to run to the cafeteria for a muffin and a cup of tea." Marti grabbed her purse. "I overslept, and I wanted to make sure David was all right before I did. I should be back in thirty minutes or so. That'll give you a few minutes to talk in private."

Watching her stepmother leave, Davida shot her father a questioning look.

"Before you decide that Marti's grown more perceptive with age," David motioned to the chair beside him. "I told her that we needed to discuss some personal issues."

"I'm sure that went over well." Davida sank into the comfortable recliner. "She never liked being out of the loop."

"It went over fine." David raised the head of his bed. "Sweetheart, you left five years ago without warning. Even Marti understands there might be leftover traumas you aren't ready to share."

"She's right," Davida agreed. "Be sure to thank her for me."

"I will." David absently picked at the sheet. "I know you can't tell me everything, and I'm not asking you to. I will tell you that Dan isn't well. He hasn't been around the office much since his retirement, so I was shocked to see him last week. He looked worse than I did during the heart attack."

"You're right," Davida agreed. "I can't tell you anything. It's been five years since I've seen Dan. I do know he was working from home a lot even before I left. Maybe he's tired. He's not a young man anymore."

"He's not old enough to look like that," David informed her. "Moving on, why don't you tell me about your meeting with Jensen. Did you work things out?"

"Yes and no." Davida contemplated exactly what she wanted to say and how she wanted to say it. "We've tentatively agreed to reconcile if we can work through the first few hurdles."

"If you can get past Jensen's sleeping around while you were separated." Her father cut to the chase. "Davi, you're the one who abandoned your vows without a backward glance. I understand emotions were high, and there were extenuating circumstances. However, there's no getting around the fact that your disappearance nearly destroyed that man." David reached out to pat her hand.

"Jensen didn't do anything but bury himself in work the first year. Maybe longer. He never looked at another woman. He kept hoping you'd change your mind and come home. Eventually, he lost hope and moved on. You can't blame him for a situation you created."

From the look on her face, she could.

"How do you think I felt?" Davida asked quietly. "He wasn't the only one hurt by Sharon's actions."

"No, he wasn't." David agreed. "But he was the one who wasn't given a chance to defend himself. You found him guilty without a trial based on shoddy evidence. If you recall, I tried to talk some sense into you at the time and for several years after. You wouldn't listen. Now I know why."

More importantly, Jensen did, too.

"I guess you do." Davida closed her eyes briefly, trying to gather her thoughts. "Jensen wasn't the only one who buried himself in his work. I don't think I pulled my head out of the emotional sand until I reached England."

"But you made quite the name for yourself along the way." He should know, he still had the newspaper clippings she'd sent him over the years. "Your Mom would be proud of you."

"I think she would be," Davida agreed. "On the professional front, at least. I'm not sure how she'd feel about my marriage."

"Like you did what you thought was best at the time." David studied his daughter. "Who knows? Things may have escalated if you'd tried to talk things through too soon. You've had time to work through your emotions. See what you've lost. That might play in your favor. We'll have to wait and see."

"In the meantime, we're supposed to bring another life into this crap storm." Davida winced at the thought. "With no guarantees we'll stay together."

"Kiddo, that's life." David grasped her hands. "Sometimes you win. Sometimes you lose. The game hasn't changed in thousands of years. While I can't tell you what to do, I can say you'll always regret not trying if you walk away. I don't want to see that happen."

"I think you're right." Davida squeezed his hand. "I have to do this even if we fail."

"I agree." While she didn't see it now, he doubted she'd fail if she kept her head out of it. "Jensen still loves you and, whether you realize it or not, some part of you still loves him."

Like the heart she protected so fiercely.

"You two were meant for each other. That's why I didn't raise holy hell when you came dragging him home. The man was my boss and a dozen years older than you."

Almost fourteen, but who was counting?

"Right." Davida rolled her eyes. "Marti is twenty years younger than you."

Closer to twenty-two, but, again, who was counting?

"While that's true, my wife was a thirty-year-old divorcee when we met and thirty-two when we married." David agreed. "You were a twenty-year-old scholar who'd never had a serious boyfriend. Bradley doesn't count. He was like you. More interested in quantum physics than he was in sex. All that changed with Jensen."

She'd started wondering what she was missing fast.

"If it makes you feel better, Jensen never tried anything while we were dating." He'd waited until they were engaged for a while. However, she wasn't going there with her dad. "I think Dan threatened to disinherit him if he did."

"You may be right." He seemed to remember his boss telling him something to that effect over after-dinner drinks. "I don't think it was necessary."

"It wasn't." Davida smiled at her memories. "We were both done by the third date."

"Third date stateside or that visit across the pond?" David was still miffed that Jensen played that card after all these years. "I'm still thinking about kicking his butt for that one."

He didn't have any doubts; that was when the bounder swept his baby off her feet.

"We were staying in a castle in Scotland." Davida ignored her father's outraged look. "Dad, I've already told you nothing happened. We had separate rooms." Jensen insisted. "But, even if we hadn't, I was a grown woman capable of making my own decisions."

David's rude snort said otherwise.

"Stop it." Davida laughed at her father. "While I didn't know it at the time, Jensen was playing the long game. In his mind, getting a wedding band on my finger far outweighed any temporary benefits that might blow the whole thing."

"He was smart." David agreed. "I wish I could say I don't know what a man like Jensen saw in a girl like you, but I do. I saw it in Luce the first day we met. She was a special woman, and while we didn't share many common interests, we'd still be together if she were alive. Never doubt that. Despite occasional tensions, we were happy together."

Davida could second that. They'd been crazy about each other. In every way. Everyone who saw them knew it wasn't an act. She'd lived with that truth every day, and she'd wanted the same for herself.

What her father called "moments" were highly combustible, surprisingly soft-spoken confrontations where one or the other had reached the end of their tolerance with their spouse's antics. Whether it was her father's epic dedication to his work or her mother's willingness to leave her family for extended periods, they'd always worked through their differences to restore harmony. As much as she blanched at the thought, it usually included a stint with her grandparents for a few days. While she now knew what that meant, the idea of her parents having sex was still a yuck moment.

"I don't think anybody would doubt that," Davida agreed. "I know how much you loved each other. I saw it every day."

"And I watched Jensen fall more in love with you every day." He'd hated every second of it. "Davi, while I wouldn't pick that man for you, I made peace with your decision a long time ago. I saw how happy you both were."

"I know you did, and we were," Davida appreciated the effort. "I never understood why you objected in the first place. I know it was more than his age."

"It was," David agreed. "I never cared that my future son-in-law would be my boss one day. I did care that he was so much more experienced than you. I won't deny that."

After watching the revolving door of lovers over the years, he'd had serious doubts about his son-in-law's integrity when his daughter initially started dating him. He'd quickly noticed the difference in how Jensen treated his daughter and knew this was more than a fling. It was more serious and less casual. While no guarantee that Davi wouldn't get hurt, she was learning to be an adult, and who she chose to date was part of it.

"Jensen went through women like water before he met you. To his credit, he kept it casual and never led anyone on. That didn't change the fact he was far too worldly for you."

He still was in a lot of ways, but she'd grown in the years they'd been apart. What she lacked in sexual experience, she made up for in life experience. She wasn't the woman who'd fled their home five years ago. He was sure of that. It wouldn't take Jensen long to realize that for himself. Turning back to her father, Davida realized David was still rambling on.

"When the boy hit his early thirties with no sign of settling down, Dan had something to say about it. Jensen spent the next couple of years auditioning suitable mates before settling on Sharon. We knew he didn't love her any more than she loved him, but they were well matched in a lot of ways."

Not the least of which was their sexual appetites. Personally, David found the woman too predatory for his tastes, even if Jensen took her confident aggression in stride. They seemed a perfect match in all the ways that mattered to their families. From looks to education to socioeconomics, they were a power couple in the making.

"While everything seemed to go well, Jensen's pride took a hit when she dumped him right before the wedding." David continued. "He came back from Monte Carlo alone and threw himself into his work for the next few weeks. If he hadn't, he wouldn't have met you."

The rest was history.

"If that's true, what was your real objection to our relationship?" Davida cocked her brow at her father in that knowing way. Jensen's worldliness wasn't the true cause, and she knew it. "I've never understood your feelings since Jensen stopped his womanizing before we met."

"You're too much like your mother and me," David finally admitted. "Too different with different interests. While Luce and I made it work, it wasn't easy. We were just too stubborn to give up when others would have thrown in the towel.

For us, our love was enough. That and we had you. For most people, it wouldn't be. I didn't want to watch you go through what we did, and I didn't want to see your pain if you failed."

"Yet you still want me to reconcile with Jensen." Davida didn't get it. "Even knowing we're probably even more different now than we were then."

"I was wrong," David stated bluntly. "Over the last five years, I've come to realize it doesn't matter how hard you work to be happy; it's worth it in the end. I also know you. You aren't a quitter, and you won't be happy unless you try again."

"I quit a long time ago," Davida reminded him. "I walked away five years ago today. Why should I try again?"

"Because you'll always wonder if you would have made it if you don't," David stated bluntly. "You might as well suck it up and use that key Jensen gave you. Confront your ghosts, admit you were wrong, and lay your resentment to rest.

I'm with Dan on this one. You need to give your marriage one last shot. If it works, make up for lost time. If it doesn't, both of you can move on knowing it was never meant to be."

"You're right," Davida rose to her feet. "Misgivings aside, I have to try."

"Yes, you do." David agreed. "We both know that."

"We do." Davida agreed. "I'm going to swing by the house on my way back to the hotel. Depending on what I find, I may check out and spend the rest of my stay there. Confront a few memories and exorcise some ghosts."

"That sounds like a good place to start," David agreed. "After that, invite Jensen to dinner. Have a glass of wine. Talk things over. Cook a meal together like you used to. Get comfortable with each other again. Be open to what you feel. You're a smart girl, Davi. Let your heart, not your head, lead you on this one. Your marriage deserves a real second chance."

"I'll try," Davida agreed. "It won't be easy."

Too much water had passed under that bridge.

"No, it won't," David agreed. "But I have confidence you can do it."

"I hope you're right." Standing up, Davida kissed her dad on the cheek. "I'll give you a call later."

"I'll be here."

David watched his daughter walk out the door as his smiling wife walked back in.

CHAPTER SEVEN

I nserting her key in the lock, Davida opened the door to her old life, not sure how to go about resurrecting a phoenix from the ashes of her past. Every good thing that made this house a home had been incinerated on a cold winter's day five years ago. She wasn't sure she could work through the cinders.

Walking through the foyer into the den, she was mildly surprised that Jensen meant what he said. Their home was exactly as she'd left it. Clean and fresh, but void of that slightly messy, lived-in feeling it once possessed. That wasn't entirely unexpected since the house was currently empty and had been for years. She knew Jensen moved out soon after she left.

He'd probably rented the house instead. That made perfect sense. It was a beautiful place. From what she could see, he'd had excellent tenants if he had. Knowing her husband, she wouldn't expect anything less. Turning at the sound of a second key in the lock, she watched her nemesis walk through the door with several bags in hand.

"I'm glad you called." He carried his bags into the kitchen to unload the groceries with a familiarity she didn't expect. "I stopped by the store on the way in."

Davida wasn't sure she felt the same. That she was glad she'd called or glad that he'd dropped by the market on the way home like he used to. It was too reminiscent of the life they'd once had, much too soon.

The one thing she did know, by the time she'd reached the hospital parking lot, the thought of facing her memories alone was more than she could bear. Feeling overwhelmed, she'd done the only thing she could do. She'd called Jensen. Reading between the lines, he'd offered to join her, and she accepted his overture.

She had no idea he'd drop by the grocer while she swung by the hotel to check out early. She'd hoped he would beat her to the house instead. She didn't want to enter the place she'd once considered hallowed ground alone. However, it didn't work out that way. Shaking her head at her naïveté, Davida no longer saw this place as a sanctuary where nothing bad touched their love. She'd learned the hard way that believing such fantasies was folly.

"I see." Davida looked around the familiar room. "The place still looks great."

"It's been well maintained." Jensen turned to face her. "I moved back into the condo after you left. It was vacant at the time, so it made sense."

Right. Davida knew what he wasn't saying. He'd moved back into his old bachelor pad since living in a luxury condo in downtown Atlanta was more conducive to his social life than a spacious estate in the burbs. It didn't hurt that he owned the place outright, so he only had to pay utilities and fees.

"I'm sure it still looks great, too." Davida smiled fondly, remembering the snazzy two-bedroom they'd shared in the early days of their marriage. "If you weren't going to sell, why didn't you rent the place? Get a return on your investment."

Common sense dictated Jensen would have sold the house about the time he'd decided to start over if he'd been able. He wasn't. Not without her signature. The deed was in both their names.

However, he'd never suggested such a thing through her attorney, and she'd never considered selling her dream home. She'd taken an out-of-sight, out-of-mind approach to her old life. If she didn't think about it, it didn't exist. House included.

"Maybe I was hoping you'd come home," He answered honestly. "When I realized you weren't, Libby and Stan moved in as I moved out. They took great care of everything until three months ago when they bought their own house."

If Davida wondered why they hadn't changed anything, he couldn't answer. He'd never told them they couldn't, and they'd never asked. So, all he could assume was they'd been fine with the décor. Not a stretch of the imagination, considering Libby and Davida shared similar tastes, and Stan was content if his wife was. She must have been, since they'd stayed four years.

All she'd ever said was that living in his house gave her a chance to develop her sense of style. She'd done a good job of it, too. From what he'd seen, their new place was quite the showplace, and the "kids" had done it on their own.

"How's your sister doing?" Davida grabbed a head of romaine and started the salad while Jensen seasoned their steaks. "The last time I saw her, she and Stan weren't even engaged."

"They were engaged all right." Jensen was amazed at how easily they fell into their old rhythm of him doing the grilling and Davida handling everything else. "They just didn't tell anyone. Not only engaged, all but living together and planning to sneak off to Vegas on their own."

Hearing Davi's laugh, he knew she was wondering why they hadn't done the same.

"Neither of them wanted the formal wedding they ended up having. Fortunately, Libby's the baby. A small, intimate ceremony was acceptable for her."

The woman behind the man, his mother, was a stickler for keeping up appearances. That meant a wedding befitting the family name. A big, fancy one if she didn't miss her guess.

"What qualifies as small and intimate in your mother's circle?" Davida snorted softly, remembering her three-hundred-plus-person event. "A hundred people?"

"More like one fifty." Jensen carried the platter towards the patio. "I went around back and started the grill before I came in, so it should be just about ready to put the steaks on."

"Let me put the salad in the refrigerator, and I'll come out with you." Davida wiped her hands on a towel before looking around. "Amend that. I'll put the rest of the groceries in the pantry first."

"Why don't you take your luggage into a bedroom and finish looking around while you're at it?" Jensen opened the sliding glass doors. "I have a couple of phone calls to make before I put the steaks on. I should be done by the time you're back."

"I can do that." She just needed to grab her weekender from the living room. "I already know which room I want."

He knew which room he wanted her to take. But she wouldn't. Taking the master suite was too much to hope for at this stage of the game. She'd likely take the next largest bedroom upstairs with the oversized bath, complete with a large soaking tub and a balcony overlooking the pool.

At least it was a bedroom now. Back in her day, it was a combination library/office filled with a large, masculine desk and built-in bookshelves with a small chaise lounge shoved in the corner. Oh, and that huge map covering one wall with all her dream digs marked with brightly colored pins. He'd unapologetically laughed his head off the first time she'd shown him the gaudy monstrosity in an otherwise stylish room.

Watching Davida walk upstairs as he stepped through the sliding glass doors, Jensen was pleased he could still predict her actions after so many years.

· · · ·

ENTERING THE BEDROOM upstairs, Davida dropped her bags on the king-sized bed, barely registering that the room looked nothing like it had. Right now, she was more concerned with getting back downstairs to fix those drinks and join Jensen before he decided to come looking for her.

In a bedroom with her husband was the last place she wanted to be. She'd rather deal with those memories in private. Setting her cosmetics bag on the bathroom countertop, she refreshed her makeup before stuffing her lipstick in her pocket and heading out the door. As much as she'd like to unpack and settle in now, it was a safer move to wait until the evening was over.

Reaching the bottom of the stairs, she couldn't resist the lure of the master suite in passing. Opening the door, she stepped inside and felt her world crumble. As much as she believed she was over the past, seeing that room frozen in time was a full-on kick in the gut. Absently resting her palm against her belly, a hollow pain ripped through her.

Touching the black and gold duvet covering the massive four-poster king-sized bed brought back memories she'd rather forget. This was where they'd once conceived a child in love and where they would conceive a child in lust if Dan got his way. The thought of going through the motions without the emotion left her cold inside. She wasn't foolish enough to call the attraction between them anything other than what it was. As much as she wished that she felt differently, she didn't. However, she still desired Jensen as much as ever. She just didn't love him anymore. Not the way she should. That was the crux of the problem.

Tearing her eyes from the bed, Davida studied the rare 17th-century Japanese porcelain vases still prominently displayed on the dresser. When Jensen found the pair at a London auction house, he knew they were the perfect first anniversary gift. While not traditional, the vases were both beautiful and old. He couldn't have chosen better. She'd gifted him with a sterling silver Regency-era calling card case to hold his Blake Enterprises business cards in return. There was no denying she'd gotten the better end of the deal.

Shaking her head free of the memories, she walked over to the walk-in closets. Throwing the doors open, she found the well-organized space completely bare. She hadn't expected that. As crazy as it sounded, she thought she'd find Jensen's clothes hanging neatly where they'd always hung. Even knowing he didn't live here anymore. It was unsettling to discover she was wrong.

Moving over to her closet, she briefly wondered if she'd find the space just as desolate. He'd probably donated her belongings to charity a long time ago. That's what she would have done in his shoes. Opening the door, she was shocked to discover her clothes still hung where she'd left them.

Not only that, her shoes, hat boxes, and handbags were still neatly spaced on the appropriate shelves. As amazing as it seemed, Jensen hadn't touched anything. Neither had his sister. Or, more likely, she'd restored their closets to how she'd found them when they moved.

However, the most surprising item in her closet was the familiar bag abandoned in a corner where she'd left it. The one that contained her cleaned, preserved wedding gown. Closing her eyes, Davida recalled the day she chose the exquisite gown. Tara and the girls had shared one of the most important moments in her life.

Shaking her head, she marveled that, while Jensen had moved on in some respects, he couldn't bring himself to empty her closet. Maybe that was a good thing. If she remembered correctly, her old wardrobe was filled with the timeless, classic pieces her in-laws favored. Those pieces would help her transition from her present life to her future life with minimal aggravation.

While she didn't mind shopping when she needed a new outfit, the prospect of restoring her wardrobe to its former glory was daunting. She had better things to do with her time. Backing out of the closet, Davida turned the light off and closed the door. She'd sort through all that later. Right now, she refused to deal with clothes or feelings. She was still too raw to contemplate where she was going or how to get there from here.

The more she was around her husband, the more it was apparent she'd made a huge mistake. She shouldn't have smacked a bandage called denial over soul wounds and moved on with moving on. Not with Jensen Blake.

CHAPTER EIGHT

What she should have done was confront him. Wade through the nightmare and face her worst fears. While things wouldn't have ended on a pleasant note, they would have been finished long ago. There was something to be said for that. She hadn't done any of that. Now she was paying for it.

Walking into the kitchen, Davida poured two glasses of iced tea, added a couple of slices of lemon to each, and set them on a tray. Opening the cupboard, she grabbed a box of crackers and a container of shrimp dip from the fridge. Spotting her favorite cheese, she added a few squares of pepper jack to the plate as well. Carrying the tray out to the patio, she watched Jensen place the steaks on the grill.

"I'm assuming you took a tour through the rest of the house?" Taking his glass, he sipped the ice-cold liquid before setting his glass aside. "I'm sure it brought back memories."

"You could say that," Davida settled in her chair. "I realized there's a lot I haven't worked through."

"I know the feeling." He bit back what he wanted to say.

Like 'Try having the only woman you've ever loved abandon you without a word.' Not surprisingly, the resentment he'd tamped down since she fled roiled back with a vengeance the minute that he learned his wife was back in town. Then again, he'd known she would be. There was no way Marti wouldn't call her, and there was no way Davida wouldn't catch the next flight home. She loved her father too much to stay away.

While he was grateful for that unexpected tip, it had taken everything he had not to drive to the hospital and lie in wait to confront her. To finally set the record straight. That was the last thing he needed to do. If he had, they likely would have made a scene before they were done. He'd pulled a few strings to get her cell number and called her instead. It wasn't that difficult.

The loop that played continually in his head was a different story. Yes, the photos looked bad. Yes, he'd been an unrepentant cad in the past. Yes, he had an intimate history with Sharon. No, he hadn't given Davida reason to believe he'd ever looked at another woman. Forget anything more.

He'd thought she knew they were best friends as well as lovers. That he hadn't wanted anyone else since the day they met. He never would. She was more than enough for him. The events that followed proved him wrong.

"We both have a lot of baggage to work through." Noting her nod, Jensen decided to voice what he felt. "It might be best if we do it together."

"Yes, we do," Davida piled shrimp dip on a cracker and offered it to him, ignoring his final remark. "My Dad's going back to work on Wednesday with his doctor's blessing, so I'm flying out Thursday morning. Friday evening at the latest." She took a bite of the cheese-laden cracker Jensen offered her. "I won't be back for at least three months. Maybe longer."

"Then I'd like to spend as much time together as possible over the next few days." Jensen turned the grill down. "I'd also like to move back into our old room while you're here. While I can't afford to be out of the office right now," She knew it was the busiest time of the year. "My evenings are yours."

He would get those precious hours of uninterrupted time, come hell or high water. He had managers in place who could handle any after-hours fires that arose until she was gone. Not that he expected to have any. He ran a tight ship.

"We can do that." She'd bend that much. "Maybe cook together." Like they used to do. "You know, I came home because I thought my father was dying. I didn't expect to learn yours was."

"Neither did I." Jensen reached for her hand. "I know this is a lot to take in." A lot more than he'd initially thought. "It is for me, too. This isn't how I wanted our reconciliation to be." Forced and unnatural. "Time constraints aside, I think we should start over. Take it slow and easy. Let things happen naturally."

"Slow and easy?" Davida laughed out loud. "I'm not sure our ideas of slow and easy are the same."

"Probably not." She knew him too well. "But they can be."

"Okay, so what are you suggesting?" Jensen would be perfectly happy putting the cart in front of the horse if she let him. The sad thing was that her libido would be, too. "Square one? Dating all over again?"

"Something like that," Jensen answered honestly. "Just knowing we're together will hold Dan at bay for a while."

Not that he wouldn't make good on his threat if they dallied too long. He'd do it from the grave if he had to. He knew his father's desires were already stated in his will. He would lose the company if Dan's wishes weren't fulfilled. The man never backed off a plan until every avenue was exhausted. He wouldn't this time either, although he might give them a reprieve on his ridiculous schedule.

"Works for me," Davida rose to her feet. "Why don't you take the steaks up while I get the salads?"

Disappearing through the sliding glass doors, she returned a few minutes later with a loaded tray overflowing with greens, Ranch dressing, and prep bowls filled with loaded baked potato toppings.

"Since I'll already be in London on business in about ten weeks," Jensen reached for the bottle of dressing. "I'd like to drop by for a visit when I'm done. I can probably stay two, maybe three days, before I have to get back."

"You've never been that interested in my work before." He'd never been interested at all. "That's a change."

"No, I wasn't, and that was my first mistake." In his defense, he'd been taking over his father's empire at the time. He hadn't been that interested in much that didn't have to do with maintaining control of the rapidly expanding international business. Or with spending the little personal time he had left with his wife, which didn't include her work. "One that I don't intend to repeat this time around."

"If that's what you want, I'd love to show you around." After she explained his sudden appearance to her team. "I can't wait to see what Leslie's been up to while I've been gone."

"You're not going to turn your dig over to your assistant when the time comes, are you?" Jensen could already see their lives getting more complicated than they already were. "You're too invested in your work."

"The short answer is yes, I will," Davida corrected. "When it's time and while I recover. I won't have a choice, will I? The long answer is I can't for long.

From what Leslie just told me, between the latest GPR images and the artifacts uncovered, we can prove the settlement is far older and at least three times larger than originally thought. That significantly alters the playing field."

Choosing her words carefully, Davida tried to be as honest as possible about her career and her commitments to Deira.

"We now have a whole new set of complications to work through with a lot of different people before we can move into Phase Two. If things play out the way they're going, I'll have plenty of time to gestate and work on writing my reports while we navigate where we go from here. If they don't, I may have to be in England pushing things along while my belly grows."

"While I'm sorry your work's potentially stalled in the not-too-distant future, I'm not sorry we're getting a second chance." Jensen set both their empty plates on the tray and carried them into the kitchen before returning to his seat. "I have more hope we can make it than I did a few minutes ago."

"You may be right," Davida tucked her leg under her and settled back in her chair. "You may be wrong. We've been feeling each other out since I got here. Now, let's get down to business."

She wasn't tired and overwhelmed anymore. Her Dad was on the road to recovery, and she'd had time to collect her thoughts. Once her head cleared, it didn't take long to realize nothing was as simple as it seemed.

CHAPTER NINE

"**G**o for it." Jensen cocked an eyebrow at her, pleased to see her fire coming back. "Say what you need to say."

"I will." Davida mentally slapped herself for thinking Jensen looked good enough to eat. "While I'm not reneging on that second chance, I'm not making any promises. The two biggest challenges we have are unresolved anger and that your threats have no sway over me."

The complacent look on Jensen's face betrayed that she hadn't said anything he didn't expect to hear. While she'd been rather docile earlier, he'd known her passivity was largely due to jetlag and trauma. He'd also known this showdown was coming. Davida's true colors would bleed through before the night was over.

"None whatsoever," Davida reiterated. "My Dad's a grown man. He broke the law. He can face the consequences." She'd already told David that as well. "I'm not surrendering my dreams because he had a stupid moment. As for Dan, I won't incubate the next Blake heir to please a dying man."

It didn't matter that she loved him like her father. No one would extort her. Not even Daniel "Bulldog" Blake. Plowing on, Davida didn't stop to breathe.

"As for us, knowing you didn't cheat while we were together doesn't make things right." Maybe it should, but it didn't. "I still don't trust you. I don't know that I ever will."

"You haven't said anything that surprises me." Jensen absently flipped his napkin. "I knew you weren't yourself when you gave in without much of a fight." That wasn't her style and never had been. "Again, if you still feel this way, why say you'll give us a chance?"

"Because I owe us that much." Her laugh was self-deprecating. "I took one look at you and realized I still have feelings divorce won't lay to rest."

"So, none of this is about anything except your need for closure?" Jensen studied her for that slight betraying tick she didn't even know she had. "To find out if there's anything left between us."

Anything strong enough to salvage from the ruins.

"Pretty much," Davida agreed. "One way or the other."

"I see." Studying her, Jensen realized how much that admission cost her. "You want me to meet you halfway without outside influences."

"Yep, just you and me," Davida agreed. "No family baggage muddying the water."

"If you mean what you say," Jensen tossed a small grey box at her. "Then you should wear those."

"You kept them?" She opened the familiar box to display her wedding bands. "I thought you'd get rid of these long before now."

"Why?" Jensen reached out to take the rings from her hand. "I always hoped you'd come home."

Finding those rings discarded on the kitchen counter, on top of that filthy gossip rag, destroyed his world. Discovering Davida didn't leave a note shattered his heart. She'd found the situation self-explanatory. He never had, and he still didn't.

"Why?" Davida parroted. "I've been gone five years."

"Because I never understood why you left in the first place." He'd put the pieces together eventually. "Or why we never tried to work things out."

"That's why you refused to sign the divorce papers after I left." She hadn't pushed because his attorney offered legal separation instead. "Because you were hoping for a face-to-face that never happened."

"Something like that," Jensen agreed. "After you refused my third overture, I moved on with my life."

Not only refused his overtures, not touched her allowance in the five years since. Not once. She'd made her way instead. That, more than anything, cemented that his wife wanted nothing more to do with him. He hadn't been prepared for that. For the fact that she'd left with nothing and never looked back.

While they were together, Davida gratefully accepted the life he'd provided. It was a nice change for a grad student who'd barely squeaked by with a part-time job and a full academic scholarship. The fact that she'd so easily given up those extra little luxuries without a second thought proved they were done. It wasn't long before he'd accepted the writing on the wall and gone back to his old ways of working hard and playing harder.

"That you did," Davida agreed. "Five, or was it six, high-profile relationships in the last five years. David tells me you never took off your wedding band."

It was eight, but he wouldn't correct her. His lady friends hung around an average of three to six months before they'd started looking for more promising prey. He didn't blame them. He wasn't good at pretending emotion he didn't feel.

"Why should I?" Jensen laid his cards on the table. "A legal separation isn't a divorce. Separate lives aside, we're still legally bound under the law."

"That's one way of looking at it." A little twisted from a moral standpoint, but still valid in his contractual world. "I'm sure your lovers appreciated your honesty."

"They appreciated that I never promised more than I was willing to give," Jensen agreed. "Wearing my wedding band kept everything in perspective for both of us."

"That's cold even for you." Davida decided she didn't like this side of her husband. "I'm surprised anyone took you up on your offer."

"You've got it all wrong," Jensen corrected. "I never made the first overture. I accepted what was freely offered."

Old money, power, and good looks were a triple threat in his circles. He had more prospects eager to heal his broken heart than he could shake a stick at. While he was willing to let them try, Jensen made sure they knew it was a lost cause from the start. Casual sex and a pretty companion for social events were a different matter.

"That doesn't surprise me." Jensen was highly desirable on several fronts. "I've seen your circle in action."

Sharon wasn't the exception to the rule. She was the rule. Her and every other woman who'd tried to sink their hooks into her husband. She'd met too many beautiful women who weren't shy when it came to getting what they wanted. A few had made it clear they weren't happy Jensen was off the market before they had a shot at him. She'd just mentally shaken her head and walked away from the fray. As strange as it seemed now, she'd never felt threatened by any of them. Not before that night. Not in any way.

"I suppose you have." He'd witnessed their cattiness in the past, and he'd watched Davida rise above it. "They thought they could make me forget I was married. I thought they were stupid for trying. I never claimed I was over you."

His tone said he still wasn't. Davida recoiled from the emotional vulnerability she'd never seen in this man. It was neither familiar nor comfortable to witness. Jensen was strong and determined. He never displayed weaknesses like this. Not even to her.

"While you never cared about my name, money, or position, those women did." Which was the main reason he didn't feel bad when the liaisons ended. "Any of them would gladly take your place on any terms I offered."

"What's that supposed to mean?" Davida didn't want to know. "David said you never lived with anyone."

"I didn't, and I never let anyone live with me." Jensen leaned forward in his chair. "Not that they wanted to. While the condo is comfortable, it reflects that I'm rarely home. If I have clean clothes, a fresh bed, and a coffee maker, I'm happy. My lady friends, not so much."

Davida didn't doubt that for a minute. Jensen was more basic in creature comforts. As long as he had a decent cup of Joe and takeout, he was done. His attitude came from years of living out of a suitcase as the international face of Blake Enterprises in his younger days. His habits hadn't changed much since becoming CEO.

"It didn't hurt that I deliberately picked career-oriented women who were as busy as I was," Jensen admitted. "I didn't want anyone constantly underfoot. I wanted companionship on demand. End of story. I was honest about that, too."

"You're lucky you didn't end up with more than you bargained for." Davida couldn't believe Jensen's bluntness. "You were a trap waiting to happen."

"No, I wasn't," Jensen denied. "I had self-control and responsibility drummed into me as a child. You know Dan would never tolerate that degree of irresponsibility."

Nodding, she knew exactly what he was alluding to, and he was right. She wouldn't be sitting here now if Jensen had ever slipped up. He hadn't, and he hadn't left their "protection" in his partner's hands either. He wasn't that stupid or casual with either his health or his reproductive capabilities.

"Davi, whatever you think, every woman I dated after you benefited from the time we spent together." Jensen held her gaze. "They all moved on to bigger and better things after we were done. You should also know I haven't bothered seeing anyone for the last six months."

Not since Lilly Eason stormed out of his life in a huff of her signature pink and white silk.

"So, you're saying you've been alone the whole time?" Davida found that hard to believe. "You suddenly went cold turkey on the whole friends with benefits gig?"

"I was tired of meaningless flings." Jensen said smirked at how stupid that sounded. "I was also so busy I didn't know which end was up."

"That's the truth of the matter," Davida smirked back, even though she was aggravated with him. "You got too busy to fool around."

"With any of them anyway," Jensen admitted. "You were the only woman I was never too busy for." That was the truth as well. "Even when you were too busy for me."

"It's a wonder we ever got together in the first place." She'd just happened to be at the right place at the right time to run into him. "And a miracle we ever got married."

"Probably," Jensen agreed. "But I wouldn't undo it. We had two and a half great years before everything went south."

"Yeah, we did." Davida rose to her feet. "Give me a minute."

Disappearing into the kitchen, she returned a few minutes later with a snifter in hand. Resuming her seat, she set the cognac on the table between them.

"Conversation getting to you?" It could be, or she might be repeating a ritual they'd shared once upon a time. Not a cognac connoisseur, she'd sneak occasional sips of his rare after-dinner drink. "It's getting to me, but I'd still like to know what happened that day."

Gulping cognac, Davida settled back in her chair and forced herself to look him in the eyes.

"On the surface, nothing that earth-shattering. I came home from school to find a magazine taped to the front door where I couldn't miss it." Davida closed her eyes briefly. "I didn't think too much about it and carried it inside to toss in the garbage. When I put my stuff on the counter, the magazine flopped over, and the cover photograph caught my eye. I couldn't believe what I saw." Davida opened her eyes to look at him. "It took my breath away."

Jensen was sure it did. He'd felt the same the first time he laid eyes on that photograph and realized what Sharon had done. While he knew she'd touched him inappropriately, he hadn't realized how overtly graphic the woman had been.

"Your picture was on the cover, and it was damning."

"I should have called you that night, but I didn't know about the photographs." Jensen absently picked at his shirttail. "I waited because I felt what Sharon did was something better explained in person. I also thought time was on my side. My dinner meeting ran late, and the club was deserted in the back where we were. I didn't think anyone saw us."

"You just thought Sharon was trying to pick up where you left off?" Davida snorted loudly. "I guess getting unapologetically handsy was one way of getting her point across."

"Perhaps, but I wasn't interested." No part of him had responded to her overture. "Sharon got the point and eventually moved on."

What he didn't know at the time was that her exit coincided with her photographer signaling their job was done. The damning scene was captured for posterity. Unfortunately, the same wasn't true for him. His job was far from done. However, he thought it was, and he'd dropped the ball royally. He knew that now.

He should have followed his gut and called Davida. He should have told her what happened. Shared his feeling that something was off about the whole encounter. He hadn't. He'd convinced himself he was overreacting instead. Sharon was being Sharon. It wasn't the first time she'd been so flagrant in public. It wouldn't be the last. He turned her down. End of story. He couldn't have been more wrong.

"I know that now." Davida resisted the urge to pat his hand. "I didn't then. I spent the next couple of hours trying to get my mind around what I was seeing. I couldn't process the thought that you'd sleep with another woman when we were so happy. It didn't make sense, so I went to my dad."

That didn't surprise him. It was what he expected her to do. David was her port in a storm and the voice of reason when she was unreasonable. Or that was the way it had been.

"Dad didn't believe any of it. He advised me to confront you when you came home. He tried his best to talk me into waiting until you did."

That was the last thing she wanted to do. It didn't take long to shut her father down. She'd then announced she was going for a drive and left. If she hadn't, she wouldn't have been alone when the unthinkable happened.

The flip side is that if she'd waited, Jensen would have been there in the hospital with her. Either during or shortly thereafter. She wasn't sure that would have been any better. She hadn't been her most rational. The miscarriage wasn't easy, and she'd had complications that resolved with minor surgery.

"I didn't listen," She admitted. "I wasn't in the best frame of mind to start with since my thesis was temporarily stalled."

While nothing new, it was unsettling when she felt she should be much farther along. Unfortunately, her research was moving at a slower pace than expected, and family obligations prevented her from using the little free time she had in her studies. While she wouldn't have objected to spending more time with her husband, it was the endless parade of social events she resented.

"Added to that, I'd been uncomfortable all day. Nothing I could put my finger on. No real pain. Just a general feeling that something wasn't right. My first mistake was that I didn't think much of it at the time. I just thought I'd overdone it."

Davida took another sip from the glass before passing it to Jensen, who looked like he needed liquid courage more than she did.

"Those pictures were the icing on the cake of an awful day." One she didn't want to recall. "While I was in the hospital recovering, I called an old advisor to ask if her offer was still open."

Jensen passed the glass back to her. Drinking wasn't the smartest move either of them could make, but there wasn't enough in that glass to get either of them tipsy. There certainly wasn't enough to impair their judgment or lower their inhibitions. Unfortunately, wishing there was didn't make it so.

"I knew you had offers on the table." She'd never hidden that. "I never knew with whom or where." He never bothered getting the details. "I never expected you to accept one."

Barking softly, Davida casually informed him, "I accepted several before I was done."

"Okay." Jensen massaged his chin. "I didn't see that coming."

"Neither did my dad." Davida shook her head. "He was clueless when I left that night to clear my head. He wasn't the only one. I was clueless as well. I fully expected to return to his house later that night, but I never made it back."

"You ended up in the hospital instead."

"I did." Davida nodded. "For several days. When I left Dad's house that first night, I wanted to drive around the back roads to clear my head. I ended up in some Emergency Room in the boonies instead."

Forcing herself to breathe, Davida hesitated a moment as she recalled that night.

"It didn't take long to find out my pain wasn't food poisoning or any of the possibilities I'd considered. However, by the time I discovered the truth, I wasn't pregnant anymore."

"You were about seven weeks along?" Jensen spoke quietly as he put two and two together. "You conceived when we went to the coast that weekend."

They'd escaped to one of the barrier islands over a long holiday weekend to get away from the pressures and reconnect. There was something invigorating about forgetting his parents, graduate school, and the office existed for a few days. More importantly, there was something about spending a few days simply enjoying each other's company without any demands that brought them closer together.

"Probably." Davida agreed, although it could have been right here in their bed the night before that trip. "It makes sense. Our schedules were so hectic that we hadn't been intimate for a while until then."

The disbelief in Jensen's eyes was very real. It was hard to accept what he was hearing. That weekend had proven special in more ways than he'd known. Despite what he'd learned, he didn't want to believe a moment so magical could turn so disastrous without any warning.

"When I was released from the hospital, I called my dad to let him know I was leaving." She'd then swung by the nearest bank to hit her savings account. The one she'd opened long before her husband entered her life. "After that, I drove to the airport, caught a flight, and never looked back." She closed her eyes for a moment before resuming her tale. "I never told Dad where I went, or what happened that night, until after I told you. He isn't good at keeping secrets, but he can't tell what he doesn't know."

Not that keeping her loss to herself had lessened the pain. It hadn't. She'd been so overwhelmed with anger and guilt that she'd buried herself in work. In the end, her single-mindedness paid off, professionally speaking. Personally, not so much.

"But you still blamed me for what happened." Her look said it all. "Davi, I would have been there through it all." He would have dropped everything and caught the next flight back. His associates would have understood. He was sure of that. "Just as I would have remained with you afterwards." The 'like I'm here now' remained unsaid.

Nodding, Davida acknowledged his words. While she'd had five years to work through her feelings, she hadn't. Not like she should have. Seeing the fresh pain in Jensen's eyes reopened old wounds. Accepting his hand, she offered what comfort she could.

"I honestly think I blamed myself more." Davida realized her words were true. "If I hadn't been so focused on finishing my dissertation, I would have realized I was pregnant and taken better care of myself. It might have made a difference."

"Maybe." Jensen spoke carefully. "Or it may have changed nothing. We'll never know." Davida nodded at his words. "What I do know is it's time to stop running and put your rings back on."

"Then you do it." Davida extended her hand, watching him slide the bands back on her finger. "I'd forgotten how beautiful they are."

"I forgot how right they look on our hands." Jensen rested his hand against hers, admiring their matching custom wedding bands. "It's good to see them together again."

Feeling trapped, Davida briefly fought the urge to hyperventilate. The familiar weight on her finger felt too real. Too binding in a way she found unsettling. Maybe her emotions were because she hadn't worn anything but gold studs and a thin gold chain since the night she fled. Or, more likely, it was the sudden reality she didn't feel naked for the first time since she tore those rings from her finger.

"Yeah, it is." Davida sounded far more confident than she felt. "I think we just jumped the first hurdle."

Holding her hand out, she silently studied the diamonds on her finger, a little sad she'd forgotten how exquisite those rings were. Forgotten how impressed she'd been that Jensen made time in his crazy schedule to sit down with a custom jeweler to design pieces so uniquely her. If possible, she'd fallen more in love with him in that moment. That he'd wanted his band to match hers was as unexpected as it was deeply moving.

"I think you're right." That she'd let him put her rings on her finger without a fight was a miracle. "Let's hope the rest are this easy."

The look in her eyes said what he already knew. Nothing about this situation was easy. Even if he tried to make it so. Glancing at his watch, Jensen decided it was time to call it a night. He didn't want to overstay his welcome. Not when he'd gained tentative reentrance into her life.

"It's getting late, and I have an early meeting." Not that early, but early enough to provide an excuse to end the evening graciously. "Let's call it a night while you still have time to settle in."

"Sounds like a plan." Davida appreciated his efforts to avoid the awkward ending they were rapidly hurtling towards. "This was nice."

To her surprise, it was. Reluctance aside, she wouldn't deny she'd enjoyed their first date. They'd both been on their best behavior, which probably accounted for the evening passing comfortably. Time would tell whether they could maintain the same degree of civility as the days wore on.

"It was." More than nice, but he wouldn't admit that yet. "If it works for you, I'll bring my things over tomorrow night after work."

A part of her wanted to say, "That soon?" Then again, they really couldn't wait. She could only stay another couple of days in the States. While she'd said she had to leave on Thursday, unless something dire happened with the dig, she could push her departure another day or two.

"That's fine." A part of her rebelled at the thought. "Around the same time?"

"Probably." Jensen agreed. "I'll check my schedule. If nothing's changed, I'll be here between six and six thirty."

Seven at the latest remained unsaid. Davi knew the score. Meetings ran over, and emergencies happened. While Jensen was often an hour or two late, he'd never missed a dinner in all the years they were together. The same would be true this time around as well.

However, decimation of the best-laid plans came with the territory. She'd taken it in stride back in the day. She could do it again. She only hoped her husband could be as gracious when she returned the favor. There were times when they didn't wrap up until late at night. Not that often, but it did happen. Usually, when she was getting ready for a meeting in London. Occasionally, it was because they were cataloging recent finds.

"Perfect." Davida ignored the brush of lips against hers. "Drive safely and I'll see you soon."

Hanging onto the door, she watched Jensen walk to his car. Catching his wave as he slid behind the wheel, Davida closed and locked the door once his headlights disappeared around the corner. Heading upstairs, she decided that a long, hot soak in a tub full of bubbles could wait. She might as well unpack before calling it a night instead.

CHAPTER TEN

Quickly hanging her clothes in the guest bedroom closet, Davida realized there was a small cache of men's clothing in one corner. Not much. Just a couple of dress shirts and a pair of dress slacks. She didn't know why they were there, nor did she care.

She'd move them downstairs into the master for Jensen to deal with. They were his since Stan was a business casual kind of guy. Exiting the room, it hit her that those pieces were hanging in that closet because Jensen had moved in here after she left. It appeared, like her, he couldn't bear to sleep in the bed they'd shared.

However, he'd had no compulsion about converting her sanctuary back into the bedroom it originally was. Not only had he abandoned clothes in the closet, but he'd also redone the room in masculine mahogany pieces and neutral shades of gray. The starkness of the décor was relieved by well-placed pops of red. While not to her taste, the beautifully appointed room bore Kaley Montgomery's distinctive thumbprint.

Giving credit where credit was due, Tara's designer had out-done herself. While nothing about the room fit her or Jensen's style, it was quintessentially her mother-in-law, right down to the color scheme. None of that was a surprise. What shocked her was how thoroughly she'd been removed from her domain in one fell swoop.

Then again, she'd erased every trace of the previous owners soon after they'd moved in. She'd also claimed a personal space where she could flee the stresses of her day. Not unlike her,

Jensen had repurposed her domain to meet his needs. The only unexpected element in the scenario was that he'd enlisted his mother's help to do it.

Hanging the clothes in Jensen's closet, she turned to take one last gaze around the bedroom, glad she wasn't sleeping here. While she'd much prefer a hotel or her old room at her father's house, that wasn't an option. She'd committed to being here, and here she would stay. However, it was taking all she had not to flee the house she'd once considered her forever home.

Despite how she felt, leaving wasn't the answer. Their reconciliation was over before it started if she couldn't confront the ghosts in this place. Exorcise them as though they'd never been. While she wasn't sure she could do what felt so impossible right now, she had to try.

Running her hand along the duvet, Davi remembered the day they purchased it at a high-end department store. They'd ignored Tara's displeasure at their refusal to use her favorite interior designer with her ever-present portfolio of custom designs. They'd wanted to strike out on their own to create something elegant and homey. Not that picture-perfect mausoleum that they would never be comfortable living in.

Besides, this was her first home as a married woman. She'd wanted their house to reflect her and Jensen as they were. Not a photoshopped public image her mother-in-law could slap on next year's Christmas card. Tara eventually got past their insubordination enough to admit they'd turned their blank canvas into an inviting home without Kaley M's assistance.

Skirting the bed, Davida exited the room before she was consumed by memories she didn't want to relive. She wasn't quite up for the mental flashbacks she feared were coming. She'd loved everything about the life she'd built with Jensen. She'd been devastated when it ended. It had taken years to get past the betrayal. Now she was wading through painful waters she'd hoped never to revisit.

Walking back upstairs, she looked around her current bedroom. She'd already put away the limited wardrobe she'd brought with her and gone through her closet. She could still wear a few of the expensive, classically tailored pants, skirts, and jackets she'd left behind if she teamed them with the fresh, stylish pieces she was sorely lacking.

The clothing issue was easy to fix once she was sure she was staying. While Tara cut her some slack with her casual wear thanks to her "masculine" profession, she wasn't nearly as lenient when it came to representing the family at more formal events. That was the cardinal rule she never compromised on. Simply stated, one didn't embarrass The Family at the Country Club or social events.

Davida decided a targeted shopping spree was on the agenda once she wrapped up her season. She could grab the necessary one-of-a-kind pieces in London or Paris on her way home. Who knew when she'd wander the Louvre again? Somehow, she doubted she and Jensen would be jetting around the globe anytime soon.

They'd be much too busy putting their day-to-day lives back together one piece at a time. Content she'd done all she could for now, Davida decided it was time for that long, hot soak in her favorite tub. She needed a brief escape from her musings. Worrying about what might never happen had quickly become a literal pain in her neck.

Walking downstairs, she wandered into the master bath and opened the linen closet. If she didn't miss her guess, she'd find a large box of candles lurking in the shadows. Spying the box on the bottom shelf, she grabbed the rosemary mint scented votives before wandering into the kitchen to pour a glass of Pinot Noir. Returning upstairs, she prepared the tub for a long, relaxing, candlelit soak. Tossing her clothes in the hamper, she slipped beneath the heated bubbles.

Closing her eyes, Davida took a deep breath and leaned back against the headrest. Between Jensen and her father, the day had been life-altering in ways she never expected. For one thing, she couldn't believe David had stooped to embezzlement. He wasn't that kind of man. She couldn't imagine the desperation that had driven him to break the law.

For another, she was drowning in emotions she never expected to feel. That was Jensen's fault. No, it was her father's fault. If he hadn't been so stupid, she could have slipped in and out of town without her husband knowing she was here. Right. In the back of her mind, she knew that thought was ridiculous.

She wouldn't be that lucky. Luck aside, their hometown, a suburb of Atlanta, was named after Jensen's great-great-whatever grandfather, so everyone knew his family and, by extension, hers. Someone, somewhere, would have seen her and spilled the beans as they had. That was a given.

However, seeing her ex in passing was far different from spending time with him. Had her father not transgressed, that's exactly what would have happened. Jensen would have called, as he had, and demanded they meet. She would have gone to his office, heard what he had to say, and told him where to stick it. He may or may not have learned of the baby they'd lost. She would have stormed away, flown home to England, served him with divorce papers, and moved on with her life.

Thanks to her father's stupidity, that wasn't happening, and she didn't like it. Not one bit. Taking a healthy swig of wine, Davida rolled it around on her tongue, savoring the deep, fruity flavors. While she wasn't much of a drinker normally, she appreciated an occasional glass of wine, and this was a particularly good vintage. It should be. Jensen bought it. Staring at her glass, she decided she needed a drink to work through this come-to-moment. Deciding she'd had enough of a soak, she rose from the tub, dried off, and headed for the bedroom.

Sliding into comfortable pajamas, she walked back into the bathroom to brush her hair. Staring at her reflection, she made a moue at the fresh freckles dotting the bridge of her nose. While Jensen claimed they were charming, she found them annoying instead. They made her look much younger than she was.

Turning away from the mirror, Davida carried her glass of wine downstairs and out to the pool deck. Sinking into a chair, she stared out over the moon-touched water, lost in thought. There was a lot to work through, starting with how she felt about Jensen. She wasn't sure. She'd compartmentalized those feelings a long time ago and never looked back. Now, she had to open an emotional box she had no intentions of ever confronting again.

Seeing the man face-to-face after years spent trying to forget him almost brought her to her knees. Seeing how good he looked was another blow. She'd gained a line or two while he'd gained that distinguished touch of gray. No wonder women were after him. He'd aged beautifully.

Snorting softly, Davida rolled her eyes. Jensen was a sexy dog, but that wasn't what drew women like flies. They flocked because he was rich and powerful. They knew his contacts could catapult them closer to whatever dream they had. While they might not win the battle in the end, being on Jensen's arm was beneficial anyway they cut it. The doors that opened were invaluable.

She snorted again, thinking that of all the beautiful women parading through his life, Jensen married her. The least appealing of them all. She still remembered the slightly cross-eyed look Tara gave her the night Jensen brought her home. Although she never said a word, she wasn't pleased, and everyone knew it.

Technically, he didn't bring her home. They met his parents at the country club. She'd been amused by the open disapproval in his mother's eyes. Tara was offended that her son was seriously interested in some ready-to-wear kid who grubbed in the dirt instead of one of the immaculately groomed, pedigreed socialites usually gracing his arm.

Adding insult to injury, not only did Davida lack proper breeding and sophistication, but she also started four-year-old kindergarten during Jensen's freshman year of college! Given his tendency to date women close to his age, the years between them were more of an obstacle than an attraction in his mother's eyes. Or it should have been.

However, the fact that she'd grown up with him on the periphery of her life meant Davida wasn't impressed by the Blake heir. Honestly, she didn't think much about him one way or the other. He was just Dan's son. Nothing more and nothing less.

She'd just as soon kick him in the knee as look at him when he was being a cocky ass.

In the end, it was that attitude that caught her husband's interest. Besides the palpable spark between them, they'd quickly discovered they genuinely enjoyed hanging out together. Eventually, Tara made peace with the idea she was here to stay and welcomed her into the fold, silently kicking and screaming in her head.

Recognizing the olive branch for the rare prize it was, Davida did her best not to let her mother-in-law down. As a result, she and Jensen had been happy for a couple of years until Sharon destroyed everything. Correction. Until she'd let her destroy everything. That was a hard admission to make and one she hadn't made before now. She'd blamed her husband for his imaginary infidelity instead.

On that unpleasant note, Davida went back inside to top off her glass before heading upstairs. Settling into bed, she leaned back against her pillows and wondered what would have happened if they'd stayed together. While the pain of losing a child would have strained their marriage, it wouldn't have broken them. She was sure of that.

Like with her parents, life would have eventually gone on. They'd probably have the family they'd wanted by now. She'd be teaching at the local university and helping Tara with philanthropic work. If she were lucky, she'd participate in a local dig here and there. While not the life she'd initially wanted, she would have been content until the kids were grown.

Besides, that was Dan's vision for them, and Jensen would have fallen in line with his father's wishes. She would have fallen in line with Jensen's. No, she would have honored the life plan they'd mapped out before they married. Her fiancé had promised not to interfere with her schooling, and she'd promised to provide the family they both wanted. He'd also promised to let her spread her wings when they were empty nesters. Setting her glass aside, Davida shook her head in resignation. While she'd moved on, the Blakes hadn't.

Placing her hands on her stomach, she wasn't sure she would have followed their wishes back then. Not totally. She'd been too excited by her chosen field. She still was, and she darned well wasn't mindlessly falling in line now. She wasn't even sure she could do what it took to procreate. Not with Jensen.

She couldn't get past the parade of women passing through his bed in her absence. Get past the reality he'd done with them what he'd done with her. Unfair or not, she felt betrayed that he could move on so easily. So what if everyone thought Jensen was a saint for waiting a year to resume his life? She didn't feel the same. He should have fought harder for what they'd had. Not signed those separation papers without a whimper. But he hadn't. He'd resumed his life without much of a fight.

She'd waited three years to date again. She hadn't even looked at another man until Tom. She probably wouldn't have looked at him if he hadn't pursued her relentlessly. He had. She'd finally agreed to dinner. One date led to another until they were comfortably companionable and a little more.

Draining her glass on that sobering thought, Davida set it aside and turned the light off. She just kept digging herself deeper into that hole. The best thing she could do at this point was call it a night and get some sleep. Even if that was easier said than done.

CHAPTER ELEVEN

Rising early, Davida was surprised by how quickly she'd drifted off when she finally settled down. She'd expected to toss and turn all night. She hadn't. Once she decided this, too, would pass, she'd found peace in the familiarity of the walls surrounding her. She'd been asleep in no time.

While the room might not look the same, it was still her happy place where she'd dreamed of living the life she'd lived the past five years and making the discoveries she'd made. Staring at the wall where her map once hung, she placed imaginary checks over several of those imaginary flags before mentally high-fiving herself for a job well done. She'd already accomplished more in the last five years than she could have ever done in her old life.

Tossing jeans and a black t-shirt on the bed, she quickly dressed and brushed her teeth. Dragging a comb through her hair, Davida bounced down the stairs and made a strong cup of coffee. She'd already let Leslie know she was probably staying stateside a couple of extra days as long as things continued going well at the site. However, that didn't mean she didn't have her finger on the pulse of her dig. She did. Speaking of that, she needed to check her texts.

Opening the screen, she skimmed her only message. Her father was waiting to be released from the hospital later today. He wanted to visit on his turf before she left. Quickly typing a response, Davida made a date to drop by her childhood home the day before she left. That would give David time to settle in and her time to get a handle on work and the Jensen thing.

In the meantime, she was tearing into one of those over-sized, fresh pumpkin muffins Jensen left behind as a bribe. Grabbing the jar of peanut butter from the pantry, it amused her how far he was willing to go to remind her of the thoughtful little things he once did to make her happy. Things he was willing to do again if she'd let him, like swinging by her favorite bakery to purchase her favorite treats on the way home. While it didn't seem like much, that detour added a good half-hour to his commute when there were bakeries much closer to home. So, it was a big thing in her eyes.

Carrying her plate over to the bar, Davida contemplated the best use of her time. While he'd bought the ingredients for dinner last night and breakfast this morning, Jensen hadn't overstepped the long-established boundaries. The kitchen was her domain except on weekends, so he'd left the actual grocery shopping to her.

So, that meant her wisest course of action was to do her running around now. That way, she could spend the rest of the day doing what she should have done all along. Work. As if she wasn't backed up enough, Leslie had emailed several new pictures to add to the stack of photos she had yet to analyze. Added to that, there was still a ton of research to do.

While she was an expert on general Anglo-Saxon history, she didn't know everything. No one did. Making things more difficult, some of the newest finds from a different area were even earlier. The size and scope of the dig seemed to grow every day. On the one hand, that was wonderful; on the other, given the recent twists and turns her life had taken, it wasn't necessarily what she wanted to hear.

TATTERED PROMISES

Feeling mildly overwhelmed, Davida ran upstairs to grab her shoes and her purse. Shopping was suddenly far more appealing than work. She knew exactly what to make for dinner, and she knew the ingredients by heart. Sliding into comfy slippers, she grabbed her crossbody and her keys before heading downstairs and out the door. A couple of thick-cut chops were calling her name.

· · · ·

PUTTING HER GROCERIES away, Davida was amazed at how quickly she'd completed her errands, including a brief detour by the hospital. Her father had kissed her cheek, reminded her to follow her heart, and sent her on her way. Undeniably trite, it was probably the most encouraging thing he could say under the circumstances, and she loved him for it.

While it felt like all those stops should have taken much longer, peak traffic hours hadn't changed, and she knew how to avoid them. Added to that, she was in the burbs. Not Atlanta proper. Not only did that make her trek easier, but it also ensured she was less likely to run into anyone she knew, and she hadn't. Thank goodness. Taking a final look around the kitchen, she headed upstairs.

Disconnecting her computer from the charger, she tucked it into her tote with her file folders and shoved her cell in her back pocket. It was past time she made up for lost time. Carrying her work out on the patio, she dropped everything on her favorite table by the pool before going back inside to make her final decaf of the day.

Grabbing the mug she'd used earlier, Davida was amazed Jensen hadn't tossed it out soon after she left. He'd given it to her two months into their relationship. Snorting at the memory, she'd expected to find something extravagant she couldn't keep in that fancy wrapped package. She'd found a generic, trademarked black and white, 'My career lies in ruins, I'm an archaeologist' mug instead.

Her heart melted instantly. She had to hand it to him. Jensen played his cards right. Buying her something uniquely hers had snagged her affections in a way an expensive bauble never could. She'd adored that mug from the start. Who was she kidding? She'd adored her husband almost from the start.

Making her coffee, she added caramel creamer and carried it outside. As much as she enjoyed her garden back home, this was still her favorite place to work. Besides enjoying the serenity of her wooded lot, she had what felt like a lifetime of bittersweet memories to keep her company. She should. They'd made good use of their secluded backyard every chance they had from the moment they moved in.

Looking around, she could almost feel the phantom caress of Jensen's talented fingers massaging the ache from her shoulders and smell the imaginary aroma wafting from their cups of fragrant hibiscus tea. Smiling softly, she acknowledged that the days they spent side by side doing what had to be done were idyllic. It didn't matter that Jensen was absorbed in contracts while she waded through moldy old texts or studied page after page of highlighted notes. They were together, and every second was precious. It was how they'd spent time together when there was no time to spare.

Shaking her thoughts, Davida checked her texts one last time before opening her computer. Amidst the junk, there were several updates from her team and one from Tom saying he missed her already. Not only that, but he'd pointedly reminded her of the night before her sudden departure. The night they'd finally all but made love. Unfortunately, a sudden, desperate telephone call interrupted the pivotal few moments that would have changed the trajectory of their relationship. While they could have ignored the ring, they hadn't. Tom's staff wouldn't interrupt their evening unless it was something only the boss could handle.

Shaking her head, Davida wasn't sure whether she was glad or sad she'd never experienced what their heated caresses promised. Now, she likely never would. Firing off an affectionate text, she'd properly deal with Tom face-to-face when she knew what an appropriate manner was. Right now, he was still her almost lover, and she wasn't about to end a good thing until she'd fully committed to the unknown.

Moving on, she sifted through the detritus, deleting the majority of emails and responding to what was left. Although the sender would feel different, anything not directly related to her dig was a waste of valuable time. Satisfied she'd taken care of "business," she turned her attention to Leslie's updates.

Well, well, they weren't all from Leslie. Tobes slipped one in when no one was looking. Clicking on the attachment, Davida blinked at the computer-generated image coming to life before her eyes. If this was good, his hands-on reconstruction would be better. Turning back to the image, she couldn't believe the sneaky little so-and-so had hijacked that skull long enough to put a face to her warlord. All off the record, of course. Then again, Leslie was probably in on it. She'd mastered plausible deniability a long time ago.

David whistled softly. Wulfgar was a handsome devil in that battle-hardened, I'd-just-as-soon-slit-your-throat-as-look-at-you barbarian warlord way. A real hottie, more Beowulf than Harold Godwinson from Toby's reconstruction. Laughing softly, she saved the image before she opened the latest photographs from the dig. As much as she'd hoped otherwise, her team had finished excavating Wulfgar's grave without her. The realization made her heart hurt.

Since she'd discovered him, she'd wanted to finish the job. That hadn't happened, and she understood why. Her absence didn't justify halting forward progress. Their season would be wrapping up soon. They needed to get as much done as possible before that happened.

Glancing at the photographs, her team had unequivocally proven their warlord was a powerful man of means. His impressive array of grave goods testified to that. They'd found several Anglo-Saxon bowls and pots, an exquisite blue glass claw beaker, scabbards, bits of jewelry and metalwork, and the pommel of a finely decorated sword.

They had also discovered the body of a young woman buried with him. Knowing what that likely meant, Davida decided to contemplate that unpleasant thought another day. She'd draw her conclusion when she was back home, where she could see the evidence for herself. Printing the pictures, she added them to a file folder and stood up.

Glancing at the time, she closed her computer and put it away. She'd been so excited by the latest update and pictures from the dig that she'd lost track of time. It didn't help that she forgot to set her alarm. As things stood, she was late starting dinner. If she hurried, she might get everything done before

TATTERED PROMISES

Jensen came home. Leaving her work on the table, she headed for the kitchen, knowing she'd return as soon as the chops were in the oven. She still had a lot of work to get done.

CHAPTER TWELVE

Mincing onions and garlic, Davida contemplated her situation yet again. It was time to accept the truth. She wasn't trapped. She could walk away and do it with a clear conscience. Move on with her life. Marry Tom and have a good life with a good man. Her father was an adult, and he was solely responsible for his mess. He, not she, should pay the price for his sins.

Adding the onions to a pan, she knew her father would suffer if she refused Jensen's demand. No, he wouldn't go to jail. Her husband was full of hot air. Blake didn't need the negative publicity tarnishing their impeccable reputation. Her father would more likely be forced into early retirement, supposedly due to his heart attack.

He'd leave Blake with a generous severance package minus what he still owed the company. Between his savings and good investments, David and Marti would be okay. If push came to shove, he could always work from home doing personal income tax. The downside, her father would never work in the corporate world again. The Blakes would ensure that. The upside was that he would be free. That was light punishment considering what he'd done.

Stuffing homemade cornbread dressing inside the chop pocket, Davida leveled with herself. As much as she didn't want to play stupid mind games or complicate her life, some perverse part of her wanted to know if the impossible was possible. If they could make it work. She suspected that part was her heart.

TATTERED PROMISES

Putting the chops in the oven, she prepped asparagus to roast and made a Caesar salad. Deciding to call it a day, she went upstairs to take a shower and change. As pleasant as working by the pool was, she felt sweaty and grimy by the end of the day.

Finishing her shower, she dressed in a silk animal print blouse and a fresh pair of jeans she'd found in a drawer. Surprisingly, both fit better than they had in the past. A few years in the field had toned her in ways she hadn't been five years ago.

Quickly reapplying her makeup and combing her hair, Davida studied her appearance. She looked cool, comfortable, and in charge. Just how she wanted to look. Satisfied with her appearance, she went back downstairs to put the finishing touches on dinner and steel herself to deal with her husband.

Correction, she was steeling herself to spend the next couple of days living with the man she'd abandoned a lifetime ago. A man she never expected to see again. Unfortunately, the time of reckoning had come. She had to confront her past and plow through issues like they didn't matter when she knew they did.

The idea of confronting the past she'd ignored for half a decade would be daunting if she'd known what was coming. She hadn't. She was blindsided by circumstances beyond her control. Snorting at her father's stupidity, Davida angrily swiped at an imaginary spot on the granite counter before turning towards the scrape of a key in the lock.

Putting her clothes away, she took a couple of deep, cleansing breaths before heading for the foyer. Plastering a smile on her face, she greeted Jensen, deliberately ignoring her racing pulse. Life wasn't fair. No man should look that delectable at the end of a long, stressful day.

Unfortunately, her husband defied reason. The man thrived on chaos. He always had. It seemed he still did. Mentally shaking herself, she noticed the stuffed weekender in his hand. He meant what he'd said. He planned to spend every possible moment with her until she left. Not exactly comfortable with the idea, she understood why they needed to spend time together, even if she didn't like it.

"I wasn't expecting you this early." Davida resisted the urge to peck his lips in greeting as she used to do.

Thank goodness she'd done her running around earlier. Dinner wouldn't even be in the oven if she hadn't. She'd never been happier that she hadn't caved to the temptation to sleep in as she'd almost done. Fortunately, the lure of lounging by the pool with her laptop without errands hanging over her head was stronger.

"My last appointment was cancelled due to a family emergency, so I cut out early." Jensen dropped a kiss on her cheek before heading towards a closed door. "I need to drop this on the bed and check my email before I do anything else."

Davida nodded to his back as he left the room. Nothing had changed in the years they'd been apart. He still followed his old routine. Unlike her, the man was neat and organized to a fault. That would probably never change. He'd spent too many years on the road to just go with the flow.

Laughing softly, Davida went through Jensen's imaginary checklist in her head. The one that didn't change even when they were on vacation. First, he'd put his belongings where they belonged. Then, he'd make sure there weren't any last-minute fires he had to put out. Lastly, he'd check his appointment schedule and look over paperwork to make sure he was ready for the following day. After that, he'd call it a night and turn his cell off. At that point, business was done for the day. The rest of the evening was theirs.

As much as Davida hated to admit it, seeing everything fall in line so predictably went a long way towards reassuring her that Jensen was more serious about their reconciliation than she was. Knowing that gave her a modicum of control. That, more than anything, gave her the emotional strength to face what they were attempting.

Walking into the kitchen, Davida checked on the stuffed pork chops baking in the oven. Since she hadn't been sure he'd get home on time, she'd picked a meal that would reheat easily. She'd never expected him to be early. From the clock on the stove, they had a good thirty minutes by the pool before dinner.

"You made stuffed pork chops?" Jensen came up beside her to rest his hand lightly on the counter. "They smell wonderful."

"I guess they do." Davida laughed softly. "It's your mom's recipe."

"I know." Jensen reached into the cabinet to remove two wine glasses. "But yours tastes better."

"Yeah?" Davida laughed again. "Don't tell Tara I tweaked her recipe. She'll never forgive me for tampering with perfection."

"I wouldn't dare." His mother would go ballistic since most of her recipes came from her great-grandmother's handwritten recipe book. "Pinot Noir or Merlot?"

"Noir." Davida watched him uncork the bottle as she returned one of the glasses to the shelf. "One glass."

Catching his quirked eyebrow, Davida nodded, reading that gesture perfectly. He was asking if she was comfortable consciously drinking from one glass rather than stress-sipping as she'd done the other night.

Briefly hesitant, Davida decided that if he could shut their problems out for the night, she could do the same. Besides, if things continued the way they were going, they'd share a lot more than a glass of wine before they were done. She might as well start getting used to the idea now.

"One glass." Jensen smiled. "I like that."

He leaned forward to drop a kiss on her brow. As much as he'd like to give her a real kiss, he knew she wouldn't go for that. Not yet. As far as his wife was concerned, they were truly starting over from square one. Like the good years never happened.

Considering he'd never stopped loving her, he didn't feel the same. He'd gladly pick up where they left off. But he couldn't do that. Not if he wanted this to work. However, knowing how he should act and doing it were two different things. He had to remember their marriage wasn't a hostile takeover. He couldn't barrel his way through roadblocks like he would a business acquisition. He had to be patient and play by Davida's rules instead. He snorted softly. That might kill him before she was done.

"Dinner will be ready in twenty minutes or so." The object of his thoughts grabbed the glass, took a sip, and leaned against the counter expectantly. "In the meantime, we can go out there to enjoy our drink."

She nodded in the direction of the patio.

"We can do that." Jensen draped his arm lightly around her shoulders. Then he escorted Davida through the French doors. "Judging by the pink on your cheeks, I'd say you spent most of the day out here working."

TATTERED PROMISES

Lifting the tote filled with papers and folders from the seat, he pulled the chair out and motioned for Davida to sit. Disappearing inside with his burden, Jensen returned a few moments later with the wine bottle in hand. Settling into the chair beside her, he reached out to take her hand.

"Why don't you fill me in on the last few years?" His voice was deceptively soft. "I know we've talked a lot in general terms. I'd like to know the details. Like how you got from here to Northumberland by way of the Russian steppes."

"What do you want to know?" Davida toyed with the wine glass. "How I got from here to Nadja's dig or what I was thinking that night?"

"Both." Jensen squeezed her hand reassuringly, knowing he'd yet to get the full story. "You said you were driving around trying to clear your head."

"I was second-guessing my decision to leave without confronting you." Davida leveled with him. "While I felt betrayed, I didn't fully accept what I saw. I wanted to believe in us and our marriage." Jensen squeezed her hand again. "I'd finally decided to come home and wait for you. Get your side of the story. You already know I ended up in the ER instead."

Sensing there was more she wanted to say, Jensen let her gather her thoughts.

"I couldn't face you after that." For a lot of reasons. "While I didn't want a baby yet, I would have been happy once it sank in."

Jensen was stunned by her confession. He'd always believed she was as eager for parenthood as he was. The truth was closer to that she'd been ambivalent, although she'd hidden it well. While willing, she wasn't ready. Not really. She was too young, too busy, too wrapped up in her new hubby to want her cocoon pierced by the pitter-patter of little feet. She just couldn't tell him how she felt. Couldn't burst that bubble of expectation she'd always known was there.

"After the miscarriage, I was in crazy land for a couple of years."

The infamous quirked brow said it all. As badly as Davida wanted to say, "Screw you," she didn't. Jensen didn't know how true her words were. She'd been a functional nutjob the whole time she made life-altering discoveries. That wasn't exactly true either. She'd only been a loon in her alone time when she wallowed in guilt, anger, and despair. That haze of hopelessness finally dissipated about the time she became immersed in Diera. She'd started to live again.

"Look, I couldn't tell you I wasn't ready for that family back then. The thought of being a mom before I knew how to be a wife scared me witless."

Seeing how every word was a punch in the gut for Jensen to hear now, she could only imagine how he would have felt back then. He'd been ready to start that family if she hadn't.

"While I didn't want to be pregnant, hearing that I was and then I wasn't in the same breath did something to me." Davida plowed on, ignoring the agony in his eyes. "I suddenly hated you in a way I'd never hated anyone. I didn't expect to, and I'm not proud of myself, but I did. For carrying on with Sharon..." Davida ignored his indignant snort.

"And for letting those photos get taken. Some part of me felt you should have guarded our marriage better. Not let the enemy in."

Her expression alternated between being faintly apologetic and faintly angry because some part of her still felt the same.

"I think I hated you more than anything for not being with me when I needed you most. The thought you would have been there if you'd known didn't cross my mind until years later. By that time, I wasn't sure you would have been."

"You *were* visiting crazy land if you believed for one minute that I would let you suffer alone." Jensen was past the point of holding his tongue any longer.

"Yeah, well, even after I came to myself, I wasn't thinking rationally where you were concerned. Not until recently." Davida reminded him. "I even hated Tara for the extra pressure she put on me to help with that stupid masquerade, knowing I was overwhelmed with school."

That made the most sense out of everything she'd just said. His mother could be overbearing when it came to the annual charity ball. It was the social event of the year, and everyone knew it. Tara wasn't about to lose that title after holding it for thirty years.

It was an unspoken rule that "the family" contributed as much of their time and energies as necessary to pull off the masquerade. No exceptions for any reason. She didn't let up until it was done and done flawlessly. That normally wasn't too much to ask. The Blakes were good to her, and Tara was a great mother-in-law. This time, being a good daughter-in-law back-fired on everyone.

"I think I hated myself more for the fleeting seconds I didn't want our baby. Then I hated myself for failing to protect it. I ate badly, worked too hard, and didn't get enough sleep. I couldn't help thinking if only I'd done things differently..."

As much as he wanted to reassure her that those feelings were probably normal, Jensen kept his mouth shut.

"I was so full of hate and guilt for so long, I don't know what I would have done or said if we'd met face-to-face. Probably something unforgivable. So, I ran as far and as fast as I could instead."

"To the Eurasian steppes."

"Yep." Davida laughed softly. "It seemed like a good idea at the time. To get as far from everyone as possible to lick my wounds in private."

Jensen shook his head in defeat. While he respected her right to her feelings, he didn't claim to understand them. However, he didn't have to. Davida's emotions were hers to work through just as his were his. There wasn't a whole lot they could do for each other right now except be here. That was something neither of them had done in the past.

"I don't believe anything you did caused it. I think it was just one of those things that would have happened regardless of what we did or didn't do." While he hoped that it was true, it was time to change the subject that was quickly becoming too raw to dwell on. "While I'm sure we'll revisit this with my parents, why don't you tell me about the warrior priestess's kurgan on the steppes instead?"

CHAPTER THIRTEEN

Dan would demand an explanation for why they separated long before he'd accept their reconciliation. That was partially his fault. He'd enlisted his father's help in trying to get those missing answers in the early days. It had frustrated both men to no end that the father couldn't get any farther than his son had.

"You want to know about the warrior priestess's kurgan on the steppes?" Davida cocked an eyebrow at him. "Who are you and what have you done with my husband?" The one who didn't care a flying flip about her amusing little hobby. "More importantly, how do you even know about that?"

"David shared the article in that archaeology magazine you sent him." Jensen smiled at her disbelief. "As much as you think otherwise, I've always respected your work even when I was too busy to show it."

Tara was the one who felt different. She felt his wife should be more vested in Blake Enterprises' philanthropic pursuits than her career. She had her degree. That was enough. She'd believed a Blake wife's first duty was to be a Blake wife. For the most part, Dan felt the same.

"I didn't know that." Davida took a sip of wine and put the glass on the table before settling back in her chair with her leg tucked beneath her. "You know that I had offers to join several digs when I finished my studies. One of those offers was with Nadja Sofka on the Eurasian steppes. Her accomplishments are legendary in archeological circles.

She's excavated kurgans and graves in the region for the past thirty years. Mainly Scythian and Sarmatian with a few Saka graves thrown in. I was lucky she trusted me to lead that secondary excavation. It was small. Just a handful of possible grave sites close enough to be loosely under her supervision. I'm grateful for that. Without the opportunity she gave me, I wouldn't be where I am today."

She'd never taken that once-in-a-lifetime opportunity for granted. Her work with Nadja made her a respected player in the global archaeological community. She would never have been considered, much less selected, to lead Diera without her accomplishments. Her current track record of history-making discoveries kept her there.

It didn't matter that her arrival freed her ex-professor to complete her excavation without the distractions of overseeing a second site. The sharing of credit would never have occurred if Nadja hadn't realized she was on the verge of a world-shaking discovery of her own. She had, and she'd seized the unexpected opportunity Davida's call represented. Fortunately, she respected her student's talent and skill enough to entrust her with an excavation dear to her heart. Because she had, they'd both benefited greatly from their collaboration.

"You wouldn't be where you are now if you weren't an exceptional archaeologist in your own right," Jensen corrected her. "Your professor allowed you to prove yourself. You did the rest. Remember that. You wouldn't have such favorable peer reviews if you weren't exceptional at what you do."

"You've done a lot more than read an article in a magazine, haven't you?" Davida's body language was mildly confrontational. "You're right, my conclusions were well received for the most part."

She'd had a couple of vocal detractors of the crackpot variety. The kind that gave archaeology a bad name. Those who made their discoveries fit their hypothesis, rather than the other way around. As far as she was concerned, their opinions didn't count. They weren't true professionals. Not the kind she, or anyone she respected, strove to be.

"Perhaps." Jensen agreed. "I may have read your dissertation and the book that followed a couple of years back."

Oh, boy, that was big. While her book would appeal to people interested in the ancient history of that region, it wasn't in Jensen's wheelhouse by any means. Why he'd take precious time out of his busy schedule to read several hundred pages about a subject that had nothing to do with business was beyond her. Her book was hardly an easy read.

"Why would you do that?" Davida absently fiddled with a tassel on a pillow, confused by his words. "We weren't together anymore."

"Because I wanted to." Jensen reluctantly admitted as he leaned forward to grasp her hand again. "And because we've never not been together in my mind. The way I saw it, you were still my wife. I was, and am, proud of you, and I never lost hope you'd come home one day."

Davida flinched at the raw pain in his eyes.

"I was also proud you'd finally accomplished your dream. Why wouldn't I be pleased to learn you'd finally earned your Ph.D.?"

Again, ahead of her projected schedule.

"Maybe because you were never interested before." He'd been supportive in a generic way. "My parents were the same way. They read each other's articles and talked about work in a general way. Mom was by Dad's side at every Blake event, and Dad accompanied her to museum events. But they both did it out of love and obligation. Not because either was interested in the other's profession."

"I'm guilty of doing the same." He saw that now. "I'm sorry I took your career for granted. I felt that being with my wife was more important than pursuing your passion. I shouldn't have been that blind."

Or selfish. He knew Davida wasn't his mother from the start. While she was content to be a wife and a mother, her first love was archaeology. It was as much a part of her as business was a part of him. It had taken their long separation to finally accept that.

"While your book isn't what I would normally read, you have a way with words. Your excitement and your experiences drew me into your account from the start. Where it should have been dry and factual, your story was fascinating. I felt I knew that woman by the time you finished her story."

It didn't hurt that a well-known forensic artist had done a beautifully realistic facial reconstruction of the priestess. She'd been a striking redhead of average height who'd died from an arrow to the back somewhere between 20 and 30 years of age.

That she was buried with both her bow and knives, combined with skeletal changes from a life spent in the saddle, suggested she was a warrior in her own right. One who likely died in battle. Religious implements found in her grave suggested she was a religious leader as well. From start to finish, his wife had spun a compelling tale of a fascinating woman who never veered from her findings into the realm of archaeological fantasy, as sometimes happened. He'd been justifiably impressed by her presentation.

"So did I," Davida agreed. "Her grave was a complex puzzle to decipher. Thank God for Nadja. I went to her with my theories, and she offered her opinions. While my dig ended up disproving her more fanciful ideas, her familiarity with the cultures helped me interpret my findings. In the end, I followed the evidence, and that was the framework of my book."

"You did a great job." Taking a sip of wine, he lifted the glass in salute. "While we didn't share that milestone the way I'd hoped we would, I was impressed with your accomplishments."

"Who are you?" Davida smirked slightly. "Not the man I married."

"He's still here," Jensen smirked back. "He just learned a thing or two in your absence."

Like his job wasn't the only one that counted, and while he'd always known it takes two to tango, he'd learned the hard way it takes two to make a marriage work.

"I'm honored." Davida tried to ignore the thumb lightly caressing her hand, sending shivers up her arm. "My work with Nadja ended the next year, so I spent a few months excavating a Merovingian cemetery in France before moving on to Macedonia.

An old friend was having surgery. He needed someone to oversee his site for a couple of months while he recovered. Since he had an experienced staff, my presence was more covering his rear than necessary. After making sure I saw and was seen, I spent most of my time documenting my earlier dig. I left seven weeks later when I was offered the Northumberland dig. My job was done. Giorgos no longer needed me. Dr. Hanson did. He showed me the ropes for a season before he retired, and I took over the site. I've been in England for a little over two years now."

"Doing a remarkable job from what I've seen." Glancing at his watch, Jensen rose to his feet. "I think it's time to take the foil off the chops and let them brown."

Nodding, Davida watched him disappear, still mildly surprised Jensen had taken an interest in her work. He hadn't done that when they were together. She was amazed he'd bothered after she left.

Then again, she wasn't. She'd been a harried grad student with big dreams back in the day. Now, she was a seasoned professional playing with the big boys. That's probably what piqued his interest again. Her husband had an innate respect for people with a proven track record.

"Those chops look and smell wonderful." Returning to his seat, Jensen studied Davida for a few minutes, deciding she hadn't changed that much over the past few years. Not physically. She still had that subtle, classic beauty he'd appreciated from the start. "They should be ready by the time we get things set up out here."

"Sounds good." Davida rose to her feet. "You get the plates down and I'll do the rest."

Silently following her inside, Jensen was mildly unsettled by how easily they'd fallen into old patterns. It was almost like the last five years never happened. But they had, and working together to get dinner on the table didn't mean all was well.

That they'd put their past behind them. He knew better. However, it was a good place to start. Watching her plate their pork chops, Jensen added the roasted asparagus to their dishes before carrying both outside.

"Do you remember the last time we did this?" Davida turned to look at him. "I think we were eating the same thing."

"I think you're right." Jensen agreed. "It was the night before I left for that last trip. You surprised me with my favorite meal." Considering the stuffing and cranberry-orange relish were labor-intensive, the dish was a rare treat back when their schedules were tight. "I think you skipped your last class to do it."

"In your dreams." Davida watched him cut into his chop. "I rescheduled a meeting with my advisor for the next day. It wasn't a big deal since he had an open slot. Even if he hadn't, I would have bailed on the appointment. I didn't want to miss one second of our last evening together."

"Neither did I." Jensen laid his knife aside. "I'm sorry it ended the way it did."

He shook his head. The evening hadn't ended badly. The whole night was wonderful from start to finish. They'd reaffirmed their love several times before passing out in a tangled cocoon of silken sheets. He still remembered the contentment he'd felt that night. He knew Davida felt the same. It was the aftermath that became a horror story.

His marriage imploded while he was out of town for the next three days. He'd discovered that when he returned home to an empty house. Not one void of belongings. Just devoid of life. If that wasn't bad enough, he was never given an opportunity for the redemption he didn't need. Not until now. When he wasn't nearly as innocent as he'd once been.

"So am I." She didn't see how it could have ended differently. "Maybe if we hadn't been so consumed with work and school,"

"We wouldn't have grown far enough apart that our marriage crumbled at the first challenge." Jensen finished for her. "You may be right. We're both guilty of being too wrapped up in our professions."

Enough so they took their relationship for granted. They'd believed they could spackle any cracks once mergers were done and degrees in hand. Neither of them anticipated the vengeful ex-fiancée lurking in the shadows, waiting to smash their bond to jagged splinters.

"Yes, we are." Davida nodded. "While I agree with you, I don't know what we do now."

"We glue our marriage back together one sliver at a time." He made it sound so simple. "We've made a good start. Things will fall in line if we continue the way we've started."

"Maybe." Davida wasn't so sure. "All we can do is try."

"And we will." Jensen grasped her hand. "We can start by meeting my parents at the club tomorrow."

"For dinner?" She wasn't sure she was ready for that. "What time? Around seven?"

That was when they met in the past.

"Sounds about right." He should be through with work by then. "I've had dinner with my parents at their place every Thursday since you left. I don't think that's wise under the circumstances, so I suggested the club. My Dad jumped at the idea. He's going stir crazy now that he isn't at the office every day."

"From what you're saying, your parents don't know about us." Davida shook her head at the confirmation in his eyes. "You want to spring this on them in a public place."

"It's for the best." In more ways than one. "While Dad will roll with it, Mom is the unknown variable."

"I'm sure Tara didn't take my defection well." Davida squirmed at the thought of confronting her mother-in-law. "I'm sure she won't accept my return without a fight."

"She didn't, and you're right." As much as he hated to agree, he wouldn't lie either. "While I think her opinion will change once she knows why you left, we need to maintain control long enough to share it."

Tara wasn't known for being passive about anything negatively affecting her family.

"I guess we do." Davida already dreaded tomorrow night. "I'd planned on spending the day with Dad. We were going to lunch at the diner, so I don't think he'll mind a quick jaunt to that little boutique on Second Street. He used to enjoy helping me choose new outfits for those charity events your mom dragged me to."

Since her MO was casual and comfy, she needed all the help she could get when it came to more formal attire. Her Dad was great with clothes. He'd dressed her mother for years. Then, he'd done the same for her. Davida knew she always looked polished and pulled together when he finished working his magic on her.

"Then he has good taste." Jensen caught her eye. "You were always the prettiest woman in the room."

"Really?"

"Yeah," Jensen spoke softly. "I'm not the only one who felt that way."

Whether she knew it or not, Tara was always impressed by how beautifully she represented the family. It wasn't just her looks, either. Davida was bright and kind. People enjoyed being around her. As firm as she could be about some things, his mother would be the first to say he was lucky Davida would have him. Or she had been before the separation. Time would tell if she still felt the same.

In the meantime, Jensen steered the conversation into safer waters. Recalling some of their more enjoyable outings was far more conducive to a pleasant evening than worrying about his mother. Even though Davida probably felt different, Tara's reaction one way or the other didn't change a thing. Not for him.

CHAPTER FOURTEEN

Staring at her reflection in the mirror, Davida decided she would do. Jeans and a floral silk peasant blouse from several years ago were good enough for now. It's not like she was attending an awards ceremony. She was meeting her dad at his favorite Greek diner in town. Just thinking of the place made her salivate.

The food was beyond delicious. So good that she already knew she would order the Greek sampler. While everything on the menu was delicious, that was her go-to dish. The one she didn't share with anyone. The dolmades and moussaka were to die for. Forget the spanakopita, pastitsio, salad, and olives. That was yummy too.

If Jensen thought he was getting one nibble of her leftovers, he had another think coming. No matter how he begged and whined. If he was lucky, she'd order a takeout sampler to share later. If he wasn't, she'd taunt him with every bite. Or maybe she wouldn't. In the past, that kind of teasing invariably led to sensual activities she wasn't ready for.

Snorting at her reflection, she grabbed her purse and keys and headed for the door. Her dad didn't know it yet, but their day was about to get more interesting before it was done. Pulling out of the driveway, she thought about the outfit she wanted for tonight. Probably a pretty, feminine dress. Maybe a dressy jumpsuit. Then again, she had Jensen's credit card, so they might as well make a day of it on his dime.

Her dad wouldn't mind helping her pick out several new outfits and some coordinating pieces to go with the pieces already in her closet. While she fully intended to take advantage of what the European shops had to offer, it was in her best interest to have a few new outfits stateside in case of emergency. Events had a habit of popping up out of nowhere in the Blake universe.

Arriving at the iconic diner, Davida pulled into the parking space beside her father's car. He'd parked far enough from the entrance to make that possible. Watching him exit the car, she thought that he looked wonderful. She'd never know he'd just had a heart attack a few days ago.

"Hey, Dad." She hugged her father. "You look great."

"I feel great." He hugged her back. "Marti sends her love. She wants you to come to dinner the next time you pass through town."

"I will," Davida promised as she walked through the door. "The next time I come home."

"So, everything's okay?" David watched her slide into the booth. "You're making headway?"

"I think so." She watched their server fill their water glasses. "Enough that I'm leaving on Saturday instead of later tonight. Leslie has everything under control, so I can take an extra day or two now that I can't in the future. We'll be too busy winding down and preparing the end-of-season presentation for the foundation to take time later. While it's just a formality, we're expected to jump through the appropriate hoops to get our next year's funding, so we do."

"But you will?" David ordered his chicken souvlaki platter and Davida's sampler before returning their menus to the server.

"Will what?" Davida took a sip of water. "Get our funding? Oh, yeah. That's not in danger. We've had an incredible season, and it's not finished yet. As long as we justify the expenditure, we get everything we need. The constant accountability got old fast, but it keeps everything above board on both sides, so I don't mind those quarterly drives down to London."

"That's good to know." David squeezed her hand. "When's your next meeting?"

"Probably in about a month." Davida laughed at the thought that someone would let her know. "I won't mind that one since I intend to put a serious dent in Jensen's credit card while I'm there."

David laughed, knowing she meant every word.

"Speaking of Jensen, how are you doing?" That was what he wanted to know. "Are you discussing the important things?"

She knew what her father was asking.

"Yeah, I think so." Davida chose her words carefully. "There's still a lot to work through, but we talked about the night I left. Jensen didn't know that Sharon set him up. He didn't know anyone had seen them, much less photographed the whole thing, so he thought he could wait until he got home to tell me what happened. It wasn't the right move, but I understand why he thought face-to-face was better."

"What about the other?" While they were in a more secluded area that had yet to fill up, he didn't want anyone to overhear more sensitive matters. "How did he handle that?"

"He's very hurt," Davida confessed. "As he should be. I didn't handle the situation well. It was the only way I could at the time, but still not appropriate."

"I'm glad you see that now." David hesitated as their server set their meals in front of them and refilled their tea before leaving. "You can't forget you aren't the only one with issues to work through. While I know you went through a rough time, you put that man through hell unfairly. Even if you couldn't stand the sight of him, you should have told your husband why you felt the way you did. You left him twisting in the wind instead."

No matter how hard he tried, some of those feelings would likely bubble up before they were done. It would with him. While Jensen was a strong man, he was human. He only hoped Davida was ready to deal with the fallout when, and if, that happened.

"You're right." Davida agreed. "I should have, and I didn't. Now we're working to get past the mistakes we both made. Jensen seems to think we can, and I'm willing to try. All either of us can say is that we'll see what happens."

"Fair enough." David removed his chicken from the skewers. "So far, so good?"

While he hadn't commented, he'd noticed she was wearing her wedding bands. That was a major step in the right direction, in his opinion.

"Yeah." Davida bit into a stuffed grape leaf. "So far, so good. I made stuffed pork chops last night. We talked about what happened that night and about my excavation on the steppes. I couldn't believe how much he knew. He said you kept him in the loop about that. Oh, and we're having dinner at the club tonight with Dan and Tara to announce our reconciliation."

"That good?" He was mildly surprised they'd go that far this early. Then again, they didn't have a choice. "I suppose you want to hit that little boutique on the corner before we finish?"

"Do you mind?" They'd planned to spend the whole day together anyway. "Did you have something you wanted to do?"

"Nope, I think it'll be fun." David eyed an anchovy on his daughter's plate. "Like old times."

"Good." She thought he'd feel that way. "Then you won't mind helping me pick out a few more pieces to leave here in case of emergency."

She already knew which outfits hanging in her closet she wanted to update, so that shouldn't take long. She'd probably add a business casual and a dressy dress, along with a drop-dead formal, to the mix just to be safe. She'd add new purses and shoes on the off chance she didn't have anything that would coordinate at home. It would be a nightmare getting ready for an event only to discover none of her accessories worked with what she intended to wear. Tara wouldn't say a word if that happened. She'd just cut the infamous stink eye across the crowded room all night.

"No, I won't." David swiped the salty fish, narrowly missing getting forked for his thievery. "I'm assuming that means you'll come home more often?"

"I'll have to." They'd never pull it off if she didn't. "Probably for a few days every few weeks when I can get away. We haven't made it that far yet."

"Jensen hits Europe every two or three months on business, so I'm assuming you'll see each other then as well."

"I think so." Davida agreed. "If he's already on the continent or in the UK, it's not that big a deal to swing by on the way home or for me to meet him in London or Paris. I honestly don't know how everything is going to work. There's still a lot to iron out, which is why I'm staying an extra day or two. I think we're both still feeling each other out. Jensen would like to pick up where we left off, like the last five years never happened. I'm nowhere near that, and I think it would be a big mistake if we did. We've agreed to take it slow and easy."

"Probably a wise move." David agreed. "However, I don't think he's lying or overestimating the depths of his feelings. It's no secret he never got over you."

"I never got over him." Davida reluctantly admitted. "I wouldn't be here if I had."

She'd be in England with Tom, sharing his life and his bed, planning their future together. In time, they'd have a family and a comfortable life doing what they both loved doing best. Added to that, they'd leave the pub together every night much as they did now. A part of her still wondered if that wasn't the better deal. While she knew she'd be happy with Tom, there were no guarantees with Jensen.

"I wondered how long it would take you to realize that." He'd wondered if she'd see it at all. "Baklava?"

"You better believe it." She hadn't had the sticky treat in years. "I need to order a takeout sampler for dinner tomorrow. Jensen will try to steal my leftovers if I don't."

"Then we'll swing by the house so you can put the box in the refrigerator." His place was on the way to the boutique, so it wasn't a problem. "I should probably order takeout for us as well. Marti will appreciate the break."

While his wife loved to cook and insisted on fixing dinner unless she worked late, they were in the middle of testing, so it wasn't as much fun as it usually was. She'd appreciate the break, and he'd appreciate spoiling her.

"Gyro platters and chocolate cream cake?" Davida laughed at his nod. "I still remember that was her favorite."

"It hasn't changed," David confirmed. "Marti's a creature of habit."

It was one of the things he loved about her. That comfortable predictability. He hadn't had that with his first wife, and it unsettled him at times. He and Marti had little routines that they both loved, like coffee on the veranda every morning and their nightly run in the neighborhood park.

"You like that." Somehow, she wasn't surprised. "Knowing Marti's waiting at home with dinner on the table and papers to grade in your study."

He'd shared insights into his new life over the years when she'd checked in from whatever dig she was working at the time.

"Yeah, I do." David dropped his card on the tray. "I'll always miss Luce, but I have a good life that I don't take for granted."

There was something wonderful about working with Marti seated in the chair across from him. Something about ending their workday and going to bed together, knowing they'd wake up the same way. The simple domesticity wouldn't have suited him in his younger years, but it did now. He was truly content in his life.

"I'm glad you're happy." She'd hoped he was. "I wouldn't want anything else for you."

"I know that." David grabbed their takeout. "I want the same for you."

"I know." Davida rose to her feet. "I'm working on it."

"I think you'll get there if you try." David followed her out of the exit. "Just don't give up when things get rough and talk to your husband instead of running away."

"I'll take that under advisement." Davi watched her dad tuck their bags in the back seat. "What do you say we swing by your place and get this show on the road?"

"Sounds like a plan." David fastened his seat belt. "We'll leave my car here until we finish shopping. We can swing back by on the way to the airport to get it." While there was plenty of parking where they were, he couldn't say the same for Gilmore's. "You can turn your car in before I take you home. Unless you have somewhere to go tomorrow, it'll save you time on Saturday."

"You don't have to do that, but it's probably a good idea. Thank you for offering." Davida pulled out of the driveway and headed for her old home, thinking she wouldn't mind being late this time. "I'm glad you and Marti kept the old place."

While she didn't blame them, that didn't alter the fact that the new wife usually wanted a new house to start her new life, if that was possible. Her dad could have easily given Marti that, but he hadn't. She wondered why.

"So am I." He hadn't given the option, and surprisingly, his wife hadn't expected it. "Marti loves the house. She always has."

Davida snorted softly. Marti loved the fact that the house was impressive, well-maintained, in an old-money neighborhood, and paid for. She also suspected her soon-to-be stepmom had sized up the current offerings and realized her husband's home was much larger, nicer, and worth a whole lot more than anything comparable on the market when they got married. Added to that, David had renovated the whole house not long after their wedding, so Marti had a voice in the changes. While not to Davida's tastes, their home was beautifully updated. More importantly, their home now suited them, and that was all that mattered. It was a beautiful place.

CHAPTER FIFTEEN

Dabbing a touch of spicy perfume on her pulse points, Davida inhaled the light fragrance, deciding her dad had good taste there, too. He'd helped her select the tiny bottle from the boutique's eclectic selection of custom fragrances. He hadn't steered her wrong. She was positive Jensen would appreciate the subtle scent, if not the cost.

Entering her closet, she glanced over her new separates. She'd spent far more than she intended. However, that didn't mean she wouldn't hit the boutiques in London and Paris. She would. She'd also make sure Jensen's eyes watered when he got the bills. It served him right. Rearranging her whole life to suit him and his family didn't come cheap. She'd remind him of that if she had to.

Moving on to the dressy dresses she'd purchased earlier, she was glad David had steered her into more adventurous waters. Yes, she'd bought the one little black dress, but even that was sexier than she usually wore. While not sure which dress she'd wear tonight, she liked all six. Torn between the crimson silk wrap dress and the animal print, she chose the pattern instead.

A few minutes later, Davida stared at her reflection in the full-length mirror, deciding she liked the stylish animal print dress coupled with the classic ruby leather pumps and matching clutch her father insisted she buy. She better. The last thing she needed was to fret about her appearance over dinner with her in-laws.

The situation was tense enough without adding the wrong outfit to the mix. If she did, she'd never live it down. She couldn't disgrace the Blakes at the country club under any circumstances. Especially not these. She still didn't get why they weren't meeting her in-laws at their place to get the worst of it out of the way before they transitioned to the country club.

On second thought, maybe she did. Jensen hoped to prevent things from spiraling out of control as they easily could. He'd made no secret of that fact. As much as she hated to admit it, his way was probably best. They should all be old enough for that not to happen. However, she was enough of a realist to know they weren't.

While not openly against her or their marriage after she accepted the inevitable, it was no secret Tara found their union marginally acceptable on a good day. Her pedigree and social standing weren't up to snuff. Not initially. Fortunately, the longer they were married, the less that seemed to matter.

However, that was before she'd done the unforgivable. How Tara would feel about their reconciliation five years after she'd deserted the Blake heir remained to be seen. She could go ballistic. Even in public. That wouldn't be a pretty sight. Shaking her fears, Davida grabbed her purse and headed for the stairs.

If she didn't miss her guess, Jensen was already downstairs contemplating how best to navigate the evening ahead of them. Entering the den, she wasn't surprised to discover she was right. What she didn't anticipate was how striking the man looked leaning against the fireplace, lost in thought. Walking over to rest her hand on his arm, Davida spoke softly.

"Hi." Her smile was gentle. "I know Tee is a force to reckon with, but we'll get through this."

"Yes, we will." Jensen agreed. "You still have this?"

He gently fingered one of her delicate diamond and ruby earrings before glancing at her neck to see the matching negligee pendant nestled against her skin.

"You didn't think I'd leave them behind?" Davida shook her head in disbelief. "You took time out of your busy schedule to find the perfect birthday gift. I'll always treasure the set."

Ignoring the unspoken 'whether we're together or not,' Jensen decided to let sleeping dogs lie. He wouldn't admit he just happened to walk by that shop on the way to a business meeting one blustery London afternoon six years ago.

Not only happened by, but happened to look in the shop window, which wasn't something he normally did. Fortunately, he had. He'd immediately known his wife would treasure the delicate Edwardian set in the gently worn original box, so he'd bought the jewelry on the spot. He hadn't been wrong. The fact that she still owned the suite testified to that fact.

"You look beautiful." Jensen continued. "You've outdone yourself."

"I hope you're right." Davida slid her arms into the jacket Jensen held up for her. "I'm not sure springing your mystery woman on your parents without warning is a good idea."

"My Dad will be thrilled." Jensen comforted her. "My mother is the unknown quantity. Meeting in a public place will help keep her in line."

"I guess it will," Davida agreed. "I still think it's dirty."

"Very." Jensen closed and locked the door behind them. "But my mother doesn't play fair where the family is concerned. She won't care you were more of a victim than I was."

"I hurt you," Davida said the words that he wouldn't. "That makes me the enemy."

"Initially." Jensen agreed. "She'll get over it once she knows what happened."

To her credit, Tara didn't hold grudges. Not usually. However, Davida had a feeling this situation might be the exception to that rule. She'd done the unthinkable and embarrassed the family. That was inexcusable under the best of circumstances. This was hardly that.

"I hope you're right." However, she'd make everyone uncomfortable until she did. "I know she'll be shocked."

"She will." Jensen closed the passenger door and walked around the car to slide into the driver's seat.

"But she won't stay that way long."

Davida nodded silently as she watched him exit their driveway and pull onto the road. The unfortunate part of the journey was the fact that their house was less than ten minutes from the clubhouse. They didn't have time to discuss much, including how best to spring their reunion on his parents. Pulling into a parking space, Jensen turned to face Davida.

"You ready?" She looked as nervous as he felt. "All we can do is walk in there together and deal with the fallout."

"That's one way to look at it." Davida wasn't sure it was that simple. "It's the only thing we can do."

"Yes, it is." Jensen walked around the car to open her door. "Besides, the longer we put this off, the harder it's going to be."

"You're right." Honestly, she'd rather go home. She wasn't crazy about the country club on a good day. "Let's get it done."

Entering the foyer hand in hand, it didn't take Jensen long to spot his parents at their usual table. Waving at Hailey in passing, he steered his wife in the right direction, deliberately ignoring the curious looks cast their way. Fortunately, it didn't take long to reach their destination. He only hoped his mother didn't forget herself. The dining room would get a show they would never forget if she did.

"Mom, Dad." Jensen nodded as he pulled Davida's chair out for her. "I hope we're not late."

He knew better. They were right on time; his parents were early. They always were.

"Davida?" Tara couldn't believe her eyes. "What are you doing here?"

"I came to see Dad," Davida said what the other woman expected to hear. "But I'm sure you already know that."

"I do." There was no point in denying the truth when they both knew better. "That doesn't explain why you're here."

The "now" remained unspoken.

"Because I asked her." Jensen's tone was firm. "And because we've reconciled."

Davida's look said, 'I wouldn't go that far.' Jensen's silent response said they needed to put their best foot forward. Present a united front. Shut his mother down before she started, and this was the only way to do it.

"I see." Tara riveted her son with her special look. "After five years of not speaking, you suddenly get back together without warning."

"Pretty much." Jensen didn't flinch from her hard perusal. "I heard Davi was in town. I asked for a meeting, and she agreed. We talked and everything fell into place."

"You met and discovered there was unfinished business between you." Dan cut in. "I'm not surprised."

They should have done that a long time ago.

"I was," Davida admitted. "I thought we were meeting to sign divorce papers." She turned to her father-in-law. "Jensen had something entirely different in mind."

From the glint in Dan's eye, he knew exactly what that something was.

"I see." Tara's tone said she didn't see at all. "I wonder how the rest of the family will feel about this."

"The girls will be happy for us," Jensen said what he already knew. They couldn't wait to catch up with Davi. "It's no secret I wanted to save my marriage if I had the chance. It's also no secret that I haven't done a good job of living that way. I gave up too soon, and I hope Davida will eventually forgive me for it."

"We both have a lot to forgive." Davida squeezed Jensen's hand under the table. Something about being cornered together brought out her protective instincts. "And a lot to work through. What matters now is we're trying."

"You aren't sure you'll do it." Tara snorted softly. "You may decide to bail."

'Like you've already done,' remained unsaid.

"Enough." Jensen's tone was dangerously quiet as he dared his mother to interrupt. "Not that it's any of your business, but you should know Davida lost the child we didn't know she carried the night she left." He rested his hand on her thigh. "She suffered alone because I was too busy taking care of Blake to take care of my wife. I don't blame her for being hurt and angry. I don't even blame her for leaving."

"Neither do I." Staring into Tara's eyes, Dan verbally supported their reunion and dared his wife to interfere. "Welcome back, my dear." He nodded in Davida's direction. "Sharon has a lot to answer for." And she would; that was a given in Dan's world. "I suppose it's good she hasn't shown her face around town for a while."

Jensen started at his father's words. They were true. He hadn't seen his old lover in six months. That meant only one thing. Sharon hadn't been home, and that was a good thing. Otherwise, she'd show up at his condo at all hours of the day and night as she'd done since Davida left. Frankly, he'd gotten tired of shutting the door in her face a long time ago.

"The last I heard, she was living in New York with an investment banker pursuing her acting career." Tara supplied the missing pieces.

She didn't have to remind anyone that it was a career that hadn't gone anywhere fast. Not for a woman convinced she'd be an A-List movie star twenty years ago when she had her first, and only, big break.

"She's had a supporting role on some nighttime drama for a couple of seasons."

"That explains it." Dan nodded. "Then I doubt she'll show her face any time soon. Not once she learns Davida is back where she belongs."

Something he fully intended to mention to Sharon's father in passing. Homer would take it from there. If he didn't miss his guess, the little diva would know five minutes after her father did. If she had one eye and half a brain, she'd stay exactly where she was. Personally, Dan wasn't sure Sharon was bright enough to do that.

Shaking his head in disgust, he silently acknowledged he'd never liked that woman in the first place. However, he wasn't about to interfere with Jensen's choice. All he cared about was his son finally settling down. Personal happiness didn't enter the equation. His family and business came first.

That included ensuring there was a next generation of Blakes at the helm of the empire. That meant finding an appropriate wife and producing offspring by an acceptable age. His son had always known what was expected of him. That he'd finally married for love was the exception, not the rule.

Despite their lengthy separation, Jensen was a lucky man. While he loved his wife and his marriage was happy, he and Tara had never had that inexplicable spark he'd seen with those two from the start. If he had anything to say about it, Sharon would pay and pay dearly for what she'd done. While his son was experienced enough to deal with whatever was thrown at him, Davida didn't deserve what happened to her.

"Sounds like a plan." Jensen nodded before turning to Davida. "We should probably change the subject. Babs is heading our way."

Glancing up, Davida saw the renowned gossip bearing down on them, intent on getting the latest scoop. If Barbara got her way, the whole town would know the runaway bride had returned to the fold via social media before their soup was served.

Feeling overwhelmed, Davida smiled at how many times they'd squeezed each other's hands under the table. The number of silent gestures they'd exchanged in secret over the past few minutes was comical. She'd laugh if she didn't want to cry. However, it wasn't all bad. She was starting to realize she wasn't alone anymore, and that felt good.

All it took was one look around the table to realize she was right. Dan and Tara were already mentally circling the wagon trains against the coming assault. While Babs was a battering ram in her pursuit of gossip, there was comfort in knowing the bullying harridan wouldn't learn anything they didn't want her to know.

CHAPTER SIXTEEN

Hearing the engine hum to life, Davida glanced briefly in Jensen's direction before staring straight ahead. As badly as she wanted to speak, she bit her tongue instead. Her husband needed to take the lead on this one. However, he wasn't ready to do so. The silence between them yawned uncomfortably. Eventually, Jensen patted her hand, signaling he was ready to talk if she was.

"I can't believe we made it through dinner without a fight." Glancing in his direction, she couldn't restrain a giggle of relief. "I am so glad that's over."

His parents were trying on a good day, but she loved them.

"So am I." Jensen pulled out of the parking lot. "My mother handled everything better than expected."

"She did." Davida turned in her seat to look at him. "And your dad looked much better than expected."

"He's doing well at the moment." Jensen agreed. "It's a good thing my parents cut back on their public appearances with Dad's retirement. It's made it possible to keep his condition under wraps."

It also kept the wolves at bay as far as Blake Enterprises was concerned. Not that anyone worried about hostile takeovers with him at the helm. The company was financially solid with a competent management team in place. They could weather any storm, including the eventual loss of his father. Shaking the thought, Jensen prayed that it wouldn't happen any time soon. As overbearing as Dan could be, he loved his father dearly.

"No one would think anything was wrong seeing him tonight." She wouldn't. "Do you think your mom will give us problems?"

Tara was deep waters and a force unto herself. While she got along with the woman, she would never presume to know what she was thinking. Jensen was a different story. He read his parents well.

"I think she's glad we're back together," Jensen responded. "Initial misgivings aside, she knew I'd married the right woman when she saw how happy we were." He glanced in her direction. "She also knew I never cheated on you. She never believed those pictures, and she felt you should have done the same." She hadn't budged from her opinion in the years since. "I think hearing the whole story put a different slant on things. Learning they'd lost the grandchild they wanted so badly was painful to hear."

He was right. Tara had vocalized her wish for grandchildren during the wedding toasts. Dan had seconded the sentiment while Jensen's sisters cast sympathetic looks their way. Davida had taken their exuberance in stride, knowing they'd have grandbabies when the timing was right.

"I'm sure it was." Her in-laws weren't as good at disguising their feelings as they thought they were. "I know your dad is happy too."

"He is." Jensen nodded as he pulled into their garage. "He always suspected there was more to the story than we knew."

"He was right." Davida opened her car door and stood up. "I couldn't face the more until now."

"When your back was against the wall." Jensen unlocked the door and escorted her inside. "While I'm not sorry you're here, I am sorry about the circumstances."

"So am I." Davida set her clutch on the counter. "However, those circumstances made this possible." She gestured between them. "You know, I'm not sure any of you get it." Crossing her arms, she leaned back into the counter and faced him head-on. "Let me set the record straight so you do."

While he was confident she wasn't going to say anything she hadn't already said, Jensen sensed Davida had reached the end of her rope with recent events. Never one to suffer in silence, she had a few things to get off her chest before they went one step further. Giving her some space, he leaned against the opposite counter, signaling the floor was hers.

"For starters, my life is in England now. I have a beautiful house I'm renting. I have a dream job for as long as I want it." Davida looked up to gauge how well he was receiving her words. "Since we just discovered Diera is much larger and more significant than we thought, I'll be involved with the site for the next twenty years." Her face was pure joy at the thought. "Every new find only proves how complex this settlement was and how much we still have to learn."

Righteous indignation aside, Jensen recognized the passionate woman he fell in love with.

"If it's the unknown royal tun that we suspect, my work will help flesh out Middle Anglo-Saxon history and fill in blanks no one was sure we'd ever fill. I won't give that up. Not for you. Not for my dad. Not for the child we might have." Her look dared him to protest her words. "Added to that, I teach at a local university and vacation on the Continent with friends a couple of times a year. This year, I'm meeting Dad and Marti in Paris for their anniversary. So, I have a great life just the way it is."

Pausing to catch her breath, she wasn't all that surprised when Jensen interrupted her.

"I do get it." He fixed her with a look she'd rarely seen. "You never intended to come home again."

Never intended to see him.

"No, I didn't," Davida confirmed his suspicions. "It didn't feel like home anymore." England did. "And I knew meeting you face-to-face would only complicate things."

"While that may be true," Jensen refused to give in to the blinding anger he felt at her words. "We needed to talk."

She owed him that much.

"Maybe." Hopping up on the counter, Davida tossed her hair, ignoring the stressed tick at the corner of his mouth. "Maybe not."

There was so much he didn't know. It was probably time to remedy that. Drive home the reality that he had the upper hand only for as long as she was willing to give it.

"Jensen, I had Edwin draw up divorce papers a while back. They're more than equitable. All I want is half the proceeds from the sale of this house. Other than that, I can support myself fine on my own."

Nothing like the style she'd enjoyed as his wife, but more than adequate for her needs. Besides, she still had the allowance she'd never touched to fall back on if she needed it. They both knew Jensen would never challenge her right to have it. He'd given it freely, and she'd chosen not to use what she didn't need.

"He's waiting for my go-ahead to send them over." Davida kept her gaze steady. "I was going to do that as soon as I got home."

She didn't flinch from the anger in his eyes.

"I also intended to take the next step with Tom as soon as those papers were in your hands. I didn't care whether you signed them or not." He needed to realize loyalty didn't equate with prudery. "Intimacy made sense. We'd been together long enough that I knew we could make it. I also knew where we'd end up."

Happily married. Tom was a local, and he respected her career. As she respected his. It was apparent that Jensen never expected to hear that. Davida shook her head. Everyone changed. He should know that. It wasn't her problem that he didn't believe she had. He needed to realize she wasn't the same woman he once knew.

She didn't need him, his money, or his family name to validate her. She never had. Tom recognized that from the start. He'd supported her work from the day they'd met. While not in Jensen's league, he was financially secure and good-looking. He was also emotionally available and family-oriented. Why wouldn't she want to build a life with him?

"If that's true, why didn't you set the record straight before now?"

"Because my romantic life was none of your business." Davida shook her head in disbelief. "And because you and my dad aren't wrong either. My emotions aren't what they should be. I see that now. I didn't before. But that doesn't mean we couldn't be happy together."

"How can you say that?" Jensen was suddenly standing much too close. "We both know you don't love him."

"I wouldn't say that either." Davida ignored the tension between them. "Maybe not like I loved you, but I do love Tom. He's a good man, and he's good to me. We get along well. He's attractive, successful, and fun. Why wouldn't I want more? Why wouldn't he want more?"

"While I'm sure he does," this was a flip he hadn't anticipated. "I didn't think you did."

"You thought wrong." Davida decided it was time to say what he didn't want to hear. "Sorry to burst your bubble, but things have gone a lot farther than that casual kiss. While we aren't sleeping together, it isn't because I'm still married."

Davida ignored the stunned look on his face.

"It's because I didn't want to start a new life without ending the old one." Her look silently conveyed that meant him. "Tom feels the same. It wasn't fair to him. Added to that, neither of us had time to devote to an intense relationship before now. However, things have heated up over the last six months. So, yes, I was ready to move on and build a new life. If we hadn't been interrupted by unavoidable circumstances, we'd already be lovers."

No one anticipated an elderly local quietly expiring among friends in his usual booth in the corner. While undoubtedly the way Old Henry would have chosen to go, his unexpected passing put a damper on their amorous intents. Her sudden departure had finished what that event started.

"Not going to happen." Davida watched Jensen warily, ignoring the dangerous aura rolling off him. "Not with Tom."

"Really?" She reveled in knowing she'd finally crawled under his skin like he'd crawled under hers. "Says who?"

"Me."

Davida closed her eyes at the feel of his lips crashing against hers. She'd wondered if Jensen was still as good a grudge-kisser as he used to be. Now she knew. He was. Maybe better. Wrapping her legs around his hips, she pulled him closer as she surrendered to the ever-deepening kiss, not sure she was glad some things hadn't changed. They'd been combustible from the start, and from what she was feeling, Jensen still found her sassy mouth...invigorating. It wasn't something he could hide.

From the way her body was responding, she still found his take-charge attitude equally stimulating. Senses overloading, she contemplated letting Jensen have his way. It wouldn't be the first time they'd made love on a kitchen counter. It probably wouldn't be the last. Only it wouldn't be making love. Far from it.

"Stop." Davida's tone froze the hand tugging insistently at her lacey panties. "As much as I want to, we can't." She gently touched his cheek. "Not when I'm all but walking out the door."

Lithe legs released his hips as she pushed gently against his chest. Stepping back, Jensen watched her button his shirt before fumbling to pull her dress together. Dragging a hand through his hair, he closed his eyes and reigned in his hormones.

Davida was right. Initiating intimacy a night or two before they spent months apart was asking for trouble. While he didn't want to take one step forward and ten steps back, he wasn't pleased to get so close to showing his wife how much he still loved her, only to get thwarted by common sense.

"Yes, you are." Reaching out, he straightened her top. "And you're right to stop us from doing something we'll both regret."

He was twisting the truth. He wouldn't regret taking her one bit. He wanted Davida back. He'd never wanted her to go in the first place. Sharon had. His wife had unwittingly fallen in with the witch's plans largely due to her youth and tragic events beyond their control.

"I am." Davida agreed. "But that doesn't mean I like it."

Now that she'd set the record straight, she didn't mind admitting her perspective had changed slightly now that they'd spent some time together. Admittedly not far enough to lose her head, but better than emotionless lust. The downside was that it would be easier to fall now. She needed to watch herself.

"Neither do I." Jensen smirked. "But, when you're right, you're right, so live with it."

Smacking his arm, Davida stuck her tongue out, knowing she only added to their frustration. Rising to her feet, she walked across the room, putting some much-needed space between them. She could practically smell the pheromones swirling around. She knew Jensen felt the same.

The one place they'd never had trouble was the bedroom. They were almost too good sexually, if that was possible. It probably was since their inherent physical compatibility led them to ignore the obvious cracks in their relationship in favor of professional matters. They'd believed their chemistry was enough to pull them through the rough spots. That attitude was woefully naïve, and the last five years proved it.

"I don't want to," Davida admitted. "But I have to. I don't think I could handle starting something we can't finish. I'd spend the next few months wondering if physical attraction is all that's left."

"That isn't true." Jensen rested his hand on her arm. "You wouldn't care about my activities since you left if it were."

He chose his words carefully, knowing his past relations were hard for Davida to swallow. While it was unreasonable to expect him to remain faithful once their marriage was over, he couldn't deny that his actions hurt her. They hurt him as well. He felt like he was betraying his wedding vows every time.

However, he'd known their union existed on borrowed time. Eventually, he'd have to sever ties with Davida, remarry, and start the family he wanted with her with someone else. As hard as he fought against that, his back was against the wall. There had to be an heir. A legitimate Blake heir. That was his most important duty and, so far, he'd failed miserably at fulfilling it.

His parents had made that clear a year after Davida left. If he wasn't willing to sire the next heir for Blake Enterprises, they weren't willing to give him the empire. They'd look outside the family for the next CEO instead. They'd gone so far as to screen resumes over the past few months. Both from within and without the company. As a result, they had several worthy candidates in mind.

With hindsight, Jensen knew he was fortunate his parents gave him a year to mourn before putting their foot down. In their eyes, he'd had a reasonable amount of time to get his emotional bearings. Now it was time to get back out there and audition the second Mrs. Blake.

Not willing to lose everything he'd worked his whole life to possess, he'd done what he had to. Consequences be damned. Considering the breadth of those auditions, he was lucky Davida was still speaking to him, much less giving him that second chance. She wouldn't be if David hadn't given him the weapon he needed to make her see the light.

"You're probably right," Davida agreed. "As interesting as all this is, it's late and I need to turn in."

More like she didn't need to keep tempting fate by remaining in his presence. It wouldn't take much for her resolve to crumble like an overbaked cookie. She'd denied her sexuality for so long, and he looked delicious. Even worse, he was that good, and she knew it.

"Yes, we do." While he agreed with her assessment, that didn't mean he wouldn't fight the urge to knock on her door for a while to come. "I hope you enjoyed tonight as much as I did."

"I did." Davida poured a glass of water. "I enjoyed seeing Tara and Dan, and I think we've made strides at starting over."

"I think so, too." Jensen nodded. "I still have some work to finish." That wasn't unusual. "I'll see you in the morning?"

"You will." Davida leaned forward. "Drive me to the airport on Saturday?"

"Gladly." Another prayer answered. "I was hoping you'd ask."

"I was hoping you could, since I returned the rental car while I was out with Dad." He'd wondered why the car wasn't in the garage. "He brought me home around four, since there isn't anywhere I need to go tomorrow. I brought a couple of Greek samplers for dinner."

"That sounds good. I forgot you were spending the day together." He'd been so busy and so apprehensive about meeting his parents, he'd forgotten she was meeting David at the diner. "I'm glad you spent time with him."

"So am I," Davida agreed. "Not seeing Dad for five years was tough." Not seeing him was tougher, but she wouldn't admit that. There were some things Jensen didn't need to know. "Have a good night and don't work too hard."

Grabbing her glass of water, she headed for the stairs, feeling Jensen's eyes on her back.

CHAPTER SEVENTEEN

Setting her glass of water on the dresser, Davida laughed at the petulant look on Jensen's face as she'd made her escape. He wasn't happy she'd halted their impassioned encounter. Unfortunately, it had to be done, and she was the one to do it. The situation was confusing enough without muddying the waters with sex. Not just sex, but great sex. The best.

Added to that, she couldn't handle the possibility of conceiving a child from a one-night stand. Especially if she decided she couldn't go through with the reconciliation. While conception wasn't likely, she had failed to pack the familiar pills in her haste to get to the airport on time. She'd realized that when she'd unpacked her toiletries at the hotel the first night. No big deal. She'd start up again when she got home. Tom would wait a few days. They'd already waited two years.

So much for how she thought it would be. Jensen had upended her best-laid plans again. Turnabout was fair play. She'd then upended his. Thank goodness sanity prevailed. Her life would be irrevocably intertwined with Jensen and the Blakes if they'd given in to lust and conceived the next heir. Whether she wanted it or not. At this point, she wasn't sure she did.

The only thing she knew for sure was that it was time to put some distance between herself and the only man who sent her libido into overdrive. She refused to consider her emotions. They were a jumbled mess. Fatherly advice aside, she was determined to use her head, not her heart, on this one.

The more she thought about Jensen hitting her from left field, the less she liked any of this. As ugly as the term "blackmail" was, there wasn't another word for Dan's machinations. Or Jensen's, for that matter. She wouldn't whitewash what either of them had done. Nor would she deny that her father's crime gave them the ammunition they needed to pull such a stunt in the first place. It was a nasty, desperate situation, no matter how you cut it.

Lost in thought, she decided a nice, long bubble bath was the perfect place to mull the facts. Leaving the tub to fill, she removed her dress and hung it back in the closet before carrying her pajamas into the bathroom. Pulling her hair into a bun, she cleaned her face before slipping beneath the bubbles. Leaning into her headrest, she closed her eyes and let the warmth flow over her for a few minutes before she resumed her thoughts.

Now that she'd calmed down some, her gut told her all wasn't lost. The facts hadn't changed over the past two days. She was still confident her father wouldn't go to jail if she reneged on being a human incubator. The Blakes were too proud of their pristine image to destroy centuries of goodwill over a foolish stunt.

The most likely outcome was that David would be forced into early retirement. If that happened, he'd leave with a generous severance package complete with the benefits he'd earned minus restitution. That was more than he deserved, in her opinion. Based on what she knew of the Blakes, she was almost willing to let him twist in the wind. Her dad was a grown man. He knew what he was doing when he ambled down a dark path he'd traveled before. Almost, but not quite.

Her father was right when he said she'd regret not giving their marriage a second chance. Regret not finding the happiness or closure that she hadn't found the first time around.

Like it or not, she would be back. She would see this situation through to the end. If that eventually included a child they shared between two continents, then so be it. Her child would love living in the village and puttering about Deira.

Laughing softly, she shook her head in resignation. It was time to let the craziness go and enjoy her bath. If she didn't miss her guess, Jensen would interrupt her quiet time before the water got cold. Shaking her head, she knew she was right. The Blakes were nothing if not persistent. Yep. He could try, but it wouldn't get him anywhere. She'd make sure of that.

· · · ·

MASSAGING SERUM INTO clean skin, Davida didn't bother looking in the mirror to see who made the noise behind her. Nor did she flinch when she was lifted to sit on the countertop yet again. It wasn't the first time Jensen had disturbed her bath, and it wouldn't be the last. Even if it was a little later than she'd expected. Wiping her hands on her towel, she wrapped her arms around his neck, accepting the desperate kisses pressed against her neck and lips.

"Did you think I wouldn't hear that squeaky step?" She laughed at his expression. "You promised to get it fixed before I left."

"Yeah, well, I thought the kids would do it." He'd forgotten all about that annoyance after he left. "It must not have bothered them as much as it bothered you."

"This isn't going to get you anywhere, you know." Davida ignored the breathiness of her voice. "I meant what I said. It's so not happening. I forgot my pills."

From the clear disappointment written across his face, Jensen's determination to seduce her died a sudden death. It was comforting to know he didn't want to risk a child any more than she did.

"Then, no, it's not." Lips against her neck, Jensen loosened her towel to display the body he'd only fantasized about for five long years. "But that doesn't mean I can't push the envelope."

"Give me something to remember when I'm gone?" Unbuttoning his shirt, Davida laughed softly as she slipped her hands beneath the fabric. "Just remember, two can play that game."

Briefly closing his eyes, Jensen savored the feel of nails gliding sensuously over skin. "I was counting on it."

"Does that mean you want that cold shower?" Hands teasing ever lower, Davida laughed at his impassioned groan as she caressed him through his clothes. "That's not like you."

"It's a small price to pay to touch you again." Lightly caressing the thighs encircling his waist, Jensen pulled her flush against his hips, relishing her answering moan. "I may die before it gets that far, but I'll die a happy man."

"Maybe I feel the same." Davida ground into his thrusts, knowing they were dancing too close to the edge. "But we can't."

From how inflamed their heated touches were getting, they were only a stroke or two from the point of no return. From letting passion reign and be damned the consequences.

"No, we can't." Jensen groaned against her shoulder.

Sitting back, she rebuttoned his shirt and straightened his clothes. Smiling ruefully, she zipped Jensen's zipper and fastened his belt before clutching her towel around her. She wasn't sure she could handle another day of his teasing before she left, but she'd enjoy trying. Hopping off the counter, she tossed the towel aside, ignoring the frustrated shake of her hands. Donning her pajamas, she flounced into the bedroom with Jensen at her heels.

"You've given me something to think about, all right." Davida plopped on her bed and drew her knees up to her chin. "You've made me wish we had a few more days to explore our relationship."

She didn't have any doubt she'd fall and fall hard if she had the opportunity. The chemistry between them was as strong as ever. She wanted Jensen as much as she always had. Maybe that was the real reason she never succumbed to Tom's advances. As much as she'd cared for the man, he never made her feel as out of control as Jensen did.

"Unfortunately, I can't stay any longer. From my most recent emails, I have a few fires to put out as soon as I get home."

"I know." Not the specifics, but how real life worked. "I won't be here anyway. I'm flying to Singapore on Sunday, then to Sydney for a week."

"Personal business or Blake Enterprises?" Knowing her husband's family, it could be one or both. "Let me guess. Singapore is family, and Sydney is company business."

"While you'd normally be right," Jensen sat beside her on the bed. "Singapore is Blake, and Sydney is an old friend's wedding."

"Craig." Davida racked her brain to remember single friends in Australia, and the cocky grazier was the only one she could think of. "I'm assuming he finally found someone."

"He reconciled with Evie right after you left." Davida wrinkled her nose at hearing that. His estranged wife was one step up from Sharon in tawdriness. "That lasted about two years."

He finally gave her the boot for good when he caught her in their bed with the family attorney. He'd returned a day early from a meeting in Queensland to celebrate their tenth anniversary."

"Ouch." Evie was a bigger piece of work than she'd known. "I'm scared to ask what happened next."

"Not much." Jensen tucked a lock behind her ear. "Craig interrupted the action, told their attorney Evie was his now, and had him draw up divorce papers then and there. Evie had no choice but to sign or risk exposure. She couldn't fight the prenup because Craig had whipped out his cell phone to catch the action in real time before either of them realized he was there."

"That's horrible." She couldn't imagine how she'd feel in a similar situation. "I know he loved her."

"He did, and he was devastated, but it wasn't the first time, so he was done." Infidelity had led to their initial separation. "I can't imagine being that stupid with a generous prenuptial on the line. Then again, Evie comes from serious money. She's set for life without Craig."

Davida nodded. While she didn't come from the kind of money Jensen did, he'd never asked for a prenup. Nor had Dan or the family lawyers. She wouldn't have married him if they had.

It didn't hurt that everyone knew she didn't marry Jensen for his bank account. She'd been oblivious to the reality of being a Blake until she became one. She'd married him for love, and she'd married him for life. Somewhere along the way, she'd lost sight of that.

"What happened to the lawyer?" From what she remembered about the other woman, Evie would have moved on like nothing happened. "Somehow, I think there's a twist to the story."

"Jason still works for Craig." Unbelievable. "He married another lawyer a couple of years later. She's a terrific woman. Liz introduced Craig to Hannah. From what I've seen, the fiancée is bright, attractive, and down-to-earth. She grew up on a cattle station, so she's perfect for him."

"Sounds like." Davida was happy for their old friend. "Give him my best."

"I will," Jensen promised. "I wish you could go. Craig would enjoy seeing you, and I know you'd like Hannah."

"Maybe we can visit them later." She was surprised at how much she wanted to see their best man and meet his new wife. "Have a second honeymoon."

If they made it that far.

"Maybe we can." Craig would love to see them. "In the meantime, I should probably let you get to sleep."

"Probably." Davida agreed. "As much as I resent all the drama, I've enjoyed our time together."

"So have I." Leaning in, Jensen dropped a kiss on her lips. "See you in the morning."

"You bet." Since he was taking the day off, they'd have breakfast and spend their last day together. "Don't forget I have to leave by six on Saturday."

"I'd already planned to hit the diner on the way in." Their favorite greasy spoon would be one more memory to cement their reunion. "His pancakes are the best."

"But you'll eat waffles." That would never change. "With dark maple syrup."

"Probably," Jensen agreed. "Or I might have biscuits with sausage gravy while you drown your stack in blueberry syrup."

"If you do, I'll steal a few bites." Again, like she always did. "You can stop with the puppy eyes. You aren't sleeping in my bed. It's much too dangerous."

She was one step away from that whole 'mistake waiting to happen' happening as it was.

"Be that way." One of them had to be strong. "Then I'll see you in the morning."

"You will." Davida tucked herself under the covers. "Now go."

She watched him exit her room before closing her eyes. In a matter of minutes, she was lost in sensuous dreams. If a few of them were erotically explicit, she wasn't telling anyone. Especially not the handsome devil starring so wickedly front and center. He'd never let her hear the end of it if she did.

CHAPTER EIGHTEEN

L ooking around her comfy house, Davida was both glad and sad to be home. She'd enjoyed her final day with Jensen. While they'd spent most of the day alone just talking and lounging, they had entertained her father and Marti by the pool for a couple of hours. David didn't fool anybody with his surprise visit. He'd wanted to see how they were getting along for himself. He'd been pleasantly surprised by the sparks between them.

After her dad and stepmom left for a romantic dinner at their favorite restaurant, she and Jensen had devoured that Greek sampler. They'd ended their evening with a full moon stroll around the neighborhood before calling it a night. Her visit had ended with an early breakfast of biscuits and sausage gravy before they'd found themselves in the airport parking lot. Unsurprisingly, Jensen refused to leave until she boarded her flight.

While she'd enjoyed that day with her family, she was glad to finally be home and alone. She was exhausted, and she still had a lot to contemplate. Both about work and her personal life. Speaking of work, her flight over had been long and uneventful. Her drive to the site was peaceful. Diera was disappointingly status quo. From Leslie's emails, she'd expected pandemonium. When she'd arrived, chaos was nowhere to be found. In her absence, misplaced paperwork was found, and excavations halted.

Far from a bad thing, her team rode out the recent bad weather, cleaning and cataloging the artifacts they'd already found. It was what they usually did in inclement weather. Nothing about that was disturbing. Just par for her universe. What was upsetting was the realization she could have stayed in Georgia two or three more days without causing Armageddon. However, no one thought to notify her that those urgent fires no longer blazed. In her team's defense, they thought they were doing her a favor.

She'd been kicking and screaming when she left. Openly declaring Atlanta was the last place she wanted to be when she should be at work. Although she'd had plenty of opportunities since, she'd never told anyone her feelings had changed. She'd wanted to keep her private life private until it couldn't be private anymore.

That she was here when she should be there was her stinking fault. Putting her suitcase away, Davida quickly changed into a pair of jeans and a cashmere sweater before ambling into the kitchen. Tired or not, Tom would be walking over the threshold any time now.

As much as she didn't want to have this conversation, she owed her boyfriend the truth as soon as possible. That meant tonight. Somehow, she doubted he'd be heartbroken by her announcement. She wasn't that torn up herself. Not really. Hearing the key in the lock, Davida walked across the living room to open the door.

"Long time, no see." She accepted the box that she already knew he was bringing. "Want a glass of wine?"

"Tea is fine." Tom kissed her cheek before lifting her hand. "Something I need to know?"

"A lot." Davida went through the motions of making tea. "This isn't exactly as it seems."

She wiggled her hand.

"Then you'll have to tell me how it is." Tom calmly removed two plates from the cabinet. "As much as you claimed to hate your husband, we both knew your marriage wasn't over yet." Even if she had convinced herself it was. "I think that's the true reason neither of us pushed for more, even though the feelings were there."

"Maybe." Davida carried their cups to the table. "All I know is I never expected this to happen." She accepted the plate of fish and chips. "I didn't intend to see Jensen when I went home. There wasn't any reason. I'd already arranged for Edwin to send divorce papers as soon as I got back. The plan was always for us to become more. You know that."

"I do, and I felt the same." He'd been willing to risk everything if she were. "However, we both knew all that could change." Davida was mildly confused that he wasn't putting up more of a fight. "It's time to say what we both know. While I won't deny we love each other or that we wouldn't be happy together, we both know we aren't necessarily in love. Not the way we should be. Nor are we the special someone we're both looking for. I don't think you disagree."

"I don't."

"I also don't think there was any chance of our relationship becoming more than it is now, emotionally speaking." Again, she couldn't deny he was right. "You've already found your someone, and I think I'm still looking."

While they were both willing to settle, and they would have been content together, their marriage would never be the union either of them hoped for. It couldn't be. One party was still in love with her husband, and the other party knew it.

"I guess I did." Davida savored a bite of perfectly cooked fish. "This is so good. Thank you."

"You're welcome." Tom reached out to lay his hand over hers. "You know, we're good, better than good, and I don't want you to think we aren't. While we didn't end up where either of us thought we would, I wouldn't undo a minute we've spent together."

"Neither would I." She meant that with all her heart. "And I don't intend to lose your friendship, whether Jensen likes it or not."

"I don't think your husband is threatened by me."

Tom laughed softly, doubting that Blake considered any man a threat. There wasn't any reason. If he were smart, he would know that. Somehow, he thought he did. "If he got you back so easily after five years apart, you were never truly gone in the first place."

Even if she thought she was.

"Maybe not." Davida dipped a chip in ketchup. "You want to know what happened, don't you?"

"Yeah, I think I do," Tom admitted. "I'm sure it's an interesting story."

While he'd known this could happen, he never believed it would. He'd let his guard down enough to think they'd finally made it past the husband lurking in the shadows. He'd been wrong, and that was a tough pill to swallow, even if he acted like it wasn't.

"It's kind of like one of those stupid crime dramas you watch on TV except no one died." Rising to her feet, Davida refilled their teacups. "As you already know, I went home because my dad had a minor heart attack. Real minor. He was home four days later."

"That's good."

"Yeah, well, it is, but what led to the heart attack isn't." She toyed with a chip. "I wasn't there two hours before Jensen was blowing up my phone demanding a face-to-face."

Davida rolled her eyes.

"That wasn't on the agenda, but I didn't have a choice. He wouldn't go away. So, I went to his office determined to confront him once and for all."

"I'm assuming it didn't work out that way." Tom sat back in his chair, cup in hand. "Is that when you realized you had unresolved feelings?"

"Hardly." Davida snorted. "That's when I realized I was mad enough to gut him with a butter knife and ask questions later."

"While I don't doubt that," Tom studied her intently. "Something unexpected happened to cause you to open the door you'd already closed."

"They caught my dad with his hand in the cookie jar." Davida looked Tom straight in the eyes. "More accurately, they caught David returning some of the money he'd embezzled from the company."

"Not what I expected to hear."

"You don't say." Davida twirled her cup. "He'd already put most of it back, but the damage was done."

"Okay." Tom scratched his head. "How does that affect you?"

"You don't know the Blakes." Davida's laugh was ugly. "They've been around a long time, and they've developed a lot of traditions. One of them is that the Blake empire passes from father to son. That tradition has remained unbroken over four hundred years."

"Again, what does that have to do with you?" Tom wasn't sure he wanted to know. "You left the fold five years ago."

"I did, but, unfortunately, I didn't sever the ties." Davida carried their empty plates to the sink. "How it affects me is I'm still legally married to Jensen, and he's the head of Blake Enterprises. Since his parents decided it's past time for him to start a family, they put their foot down. My husband has a year to settle down and produce the next Blake heir or lose the company he's run for the past six years.

"So, threatened with losing everything he worked for, he decided you were the path of least resistance."

"That's what I thought at first." Davida nursed her tea. "It's more complicated than that."

"You finally told him about the miscarriage." Tom saw her flinch. "And found out things weren't as cut and dried as they seemed."

"Something like that." Davida took a deep breath. "He was deeply hurt that I kept that from him, and he was angry that he never got the chance to set the record straight. However, that didn't stop him from letting me know my dad would go to jail if I didn't fall in line."

"You told him no."

"Basically," Davida agreed. "However, as offensive as all that was, it didn't change the fact I still had feelings I never knew I had."

"So, you decided to give him a second chance."

"Not exactly." Davida closed her eyes. "Not at first. I told him how much I didn't want things to work out between us. However, once my dad confirmed he was guilty as charged, I agreed to give us a shot."

Tom saluted her with his cup. "I'm sure you gave him hell for the blackmail."

"In my way," Davida smirked. "I informed him that my father wasn't paying back the rest of the money, and he wasn't losing his job or his benefits. He could take it or leave it, but that was that. I also told him to arrest him if he stepped out of line again. Jensen agreed."

"You trust your dad."

"Oh, yeah." She truly did. "If I'm wrong, he'll go to jail no questions asked, and I'll let him."

Rising to put their empty plates in the sink, Davida reined in the panic she felt at that possibility. Sitting back down, she resumed their conversation.

"My dad's not an embezzler. He worked too hard to maintain his reputation." That much was true. "He's not a gambler either. Not usually. I've only known him to do that twice in his life, and both were the result of cataclysmic changes in his personal life."

As far as she was concerned, losing Luce and getting remarried both fell into that category.

"I don't see that happening again. He and Marti have a great marriage, so that isn't what started him gambling. Not directly. His guilt over getting remarried did." Davida shook her head. "As if my mom wouldn't be happy that he found love again. He'd mourned long enough. I appreciated he wasn't alone when I left."

"So, what you're saying is your father handled a normal emotion foolishly." Tom saw where that could happen. Unlike most, he knew the rest of the story. David should have been driving that car instead of her mother. A sudden emergency at the office caused a change in plans. Luce had run to the grocery store instead, and the rest was history. "I can see where he might." Switching gears, he asked what he wanted to know. "How much did finding out what happened that night change your mind about the divorce?"

"Not that much when I thought about all the women passing through Jensen's bed the last five years," Davida admitted. "Then, I knew I was in trouble when I realized that bothered me. What I felt wasn't that whole 'how dare he do something I haven't done' petty garbage I should have felt. It was the same gut-wrenching agony from the night I left so suddenly."

Watching the emotions play over her face, Tom was glad he'd followed his instincts. As much as he'd wanted this woman, he'd sensed there was too much unresolved baggage for her to move on. So, in the name of self-protection, he'd decided to dive in so deep and no further. He'd also decided to enjoy their time together for as long as it lasted.

Looking at Davida now, he didn't regret his decision. He'd grown a lot as she had. They both had more to offer than either of them had when they met. He'd learned how to relate effectively with the kind of strong professional he was attracted to, and Davida had grown more confident in herself as a woman.

"Then you've made the right decision." Tom gently held her hand, admiring the beautiful rings on her finger. "Your Dad was right. If you don't do this, you'll regret not trying for the rest of your life."

"I know," Davida agreed. "But I don't have to like it."

"No, you don't." As much as he wanted to say, 'Give him hell,' it wasn't necessary. She already was. "If you ever doubted his feelings, don't. Cost aside, no man puts this much thought and time into designing something for a woman he doesn't love. If you wonder if he still loves you, he does. He wouldn't have kept your rings if he didn't."

No way. Not a bottom-line businessman like Jensen Blake. He would have sold them long ago. Recouped as much of his loss as he could and moved on. Tom shook his head, recalling the hours he'd spent learning everything he could about his rival in those early days. To his surprise, it was quite a bit.

To his credit, he hadn't felt inferior to the other man. He was successful in his own right, and Davida didn't care about money. If she had, she would have touched her allowance a long time ago. She hadn't. She took pleasure in making her way.

Beyond that, he'd realized early on the only real danger to their budding relationship was his girlfriend's unresolved feelings towards her husband. Not the marriage, the man. As it turned out, he was right, and there wasn't anything he could do about that.

"I guess." She knew Tom's take on the situation was accurate. "I just wish things were different. I've enjoyed tonight. Not what I've had to do or parts of the conversation. Just being in your company. I always have."

"I feel the same." He squeezed her hand reassuringly, much as Jensen did. "However, we both knew this day might come, and I'm happy for you. I'm confident that if you get your head out of the way, you'll make it. When that happens, you'll be glad you did."

He didn't doubt for one minute that she'd have the job, the man, and the family she'd always wanted. While a part of him was sad that it wouldn't happen with him, another was already contemplating a growing attraction he'd rightly ignored. He'd always believed that when one door closed, another opened. Even in this situation.

"You're probably right." Davida laughed out loud. "But you know me. There's no way I'm going down without a fight. Jensen doesn't expect anything less."

"I'm sure he doesn't." Huffing softly, Tom was glad he'd only known the kinder, gentler Davida. He had a feeling the feisty version was more woman than he wanted to handle. "From the looks of you, it's time to call it a night. You can barely keep your eyes open."

"You're right." Davida rose to her feet. "I'm going to miss you."

"No, you're not." Tom corrected as he headed towards the door. "I'm not going anywhere."

"Good." Davida leaned on the door. "Are you heading back to the pub?"

"I think so." Tom nodded. "Jim could probably use a hand closing down."

"Okay." She nodded. "Drive safely."

Tom waved as he watched her close and lock the door before heading down the lane. Glancing at the clock, he decided Jim could handle the pub on his own for a little while longer. Right now, he felt compelled to run these latest events by Leslie. It wasn't like she wasn't familiar with the situation. She'd been his sounding board since before he started dating her boss.

CHAPTER NINETEEN

C limbing out of the trench she'd spent several days excavating, Davida stood up and wiped her hands on her slacks. Turning to evaluate the site from a different perspective, she couldn't believe her eyes. Taking in what was left of a carved wooden panel, she had a good idea what she was looking at. If her impression panned out, they'd stumbled on an Anglo-Saxon bed burial. She had a lot more work to do before she could say that conclusively.

However, from the cleat she held between her fingers and the iron fixtures and fittings outlining a rough rectangular shape, she'd bet her degrees she was right. While she'd expected to find another grave since they were excavating a small burial plot, she never expected a discovery like this. Even more important than Wulfgar, this one changed everything. While bed burials across the continent contained men, women, and children, here in the UK, they were almost exclusively Christian women. From what she could see, this burial was the rare exception to that rule.

"Hey, Dav." Leslie's voice jarred her from her thoughts. "You have company." She nodded in the direction of the dark-haired man following her. "He claims to be your husband."

From the mirth in her voice, her cohort knew darn well who was trotting behind her like a well-trained pony. No doubt she'd demanded his ID before he'd set foot on the site. While locals dropped by frequently to discuss the latest finds, unaccompanied tourists weren't that common.

"He claims right." Rising to her feet, Davida continued as though Jensen wasn't there. "And he's three days early."

She should have expected this. The man had kept her off kilter for the past few weeks without even trying. Then again, he always had. Why should now be any different?

"My meetings finished early." Jensen dropped a kiss on her cheek. "Since there wasn't any reason to stay in London, I headed your way." He couldn't wait to see her again. "I hope it's not a problem. I tried to give you a heads up, but the signal didn't go through."

"It's fine." While a part of her wanted to resent the unexpected intrusion, she was glad to see him. "My phone doesn't always work out here." Or, she just hadn't heard it. "Let me introduce you to the team before I show you our latest discovery."

Making the rounds, starting with Leslie, Davida introduced Jensen to everyone from her student assistants to the volunteers sifting through piles of dirt. Thomas could wait until tonight when everyone met at the pub for dinner.

While they'd both moved on, she wasn't looking forward to the coming confrontation. The introductions would be awkward at best, although she and Tom were fine. As she'd expected, neither of them was devastated by their breakup. Truthfully, her ex had moved on insultingly fast.

He and Leslie were already hot and heavy in a way they'd never been. Not that she had any room to talk. Or begrudged them their happiness. She'd moved on first. Turning her attention to her husband, she led Jensen back to the grave site.

"I didn't realize your site was this big." He'd never really thought about it. "Or your staff this large?"

"You thought I was exaggerating the importance of Deira." She didn't blame him. "You were never interested in my work." Davida restated the truths they both knew. "You didn't have time if you had been."

"I should have made time." Jensen nodded, acknowledging his mistake. "Like I did for other things."

"Probably." Davida agreed. "I was too busy with my thesis to care either way."

While that wasn't strictly true, she'd let that grievance go. She couldn't dwell on the fact that Jensen viewed her career as more of a hobby than a legitimate profession. Besides, all she'd cared about at the time was that he didn't interfere with her studies. She had a degree to earn and a self-imposed time-frame in which to reach her goal. She'd been well on her way to achieving that when they'd wed.

The way her husband saw it back in the day, her degree was superfluous. He made more than enough to care for his family. For the most part, he was glad she had something to keep her occupied while he was at work. Besides, her studies would fall by the wayside once the babies came. Right. Hopefully, the past five years have shown the error of his ways.

"While that may be true, a lot of things have changed since then." Like his workload and his attitude towards his marriage. "I'm interested now."

"Good, because it'll be a while before I can leave." Davida glanced at Jensen, noting he'd been smart enough to dress comfortably rather than appear in the usual business suit. "While I don't think we'll finish with Stanley here for a few more hours," she motioned towards the skeleton the team had dubbed

"Aethelstan" after the Anglo-Saxon king. "You can hang out with me, or Leslie can take you to the manor."

"I think I'd like to watch you work." Maybe get his hands dirty. "I've never seen an archaeologist in action before."

"Well, you're in luck." Davida knelt by the grave. "While I think our friend here is possibly a young male based on the grave goods and his pelvis, most bed burials are female." The remnants of his tunic and trousers were masculine as well. "Our Aethelstan could be an Aethelflaed even with that sword and helmet resting by his side. We may have a female warrior or a female warrior masquerading as a male. It wouldn't be the first time we've seen something like that. I won't know for sure until we get the skeleton back to the lab for a closer examination. Either way, this is an incredible find."

The grave goods alone were phenomenal.

"What I do know for certain is this was a high-ranking individual based on what we've uncovered so far."

High-ranking enough to give Sutton Hoo a run for its money in some ways, though not in others. A bed burial couldn't trump a ship burial in any universe. However, Stanley was more than a mere warlord as Wulfgar had been. He was royal. Most likely the son or daughter of an early king who died young.

"One of those things is this sword." She pointed to the partially exposed metal that was the edge of a beautifully crafted weapon. "Very few swords like this were buried with their owners by this time. They were so expensive that they were usually handed down from generation to generation instead." Davida pointed to one end of the sword. "This weapon is particularly fine. The pommel is gorgeous. I'd guess it's bronze overlaid with gold, inset with garnets, since we've seen that before. I'll know for sure when we get the artifacts cleaned up and tested. Right now, I can't move anything until the area is fully excavated and documented."

Leslie had already taken the preliminary photos while she'd completed the initial sketches. But they still had a lot of work to do. They wouldn't be done before dark if everything went well. If they ran into problems, it could be much later. Her husband would just have to roll with it. Frequent delays came with the territory. If they rushed, they'd risk damaging irreplaceable artifacts, and she couldn't allow that to happen.

While Jensen was seeing her world in action for the first time, she did this every day because she loved it. If he wanted her back, he'd learn to love it too. He didn't have a choice. Her career and her devotion to this site weren't negotiable in any universe. Certainly not in his.

"What can I do to help?" Surprised by the question, Davida turned to study Jensen, noting he wasn't just casually, but appropriately, dressed right down to comfortable, durable shoes. "Tell me and I'll do what I can."

"You can watch me, or you can help the kids over there." She nodded towards the volunteers manning the sifting screens. "However, I think you'll find the GPR more interesting. Jeremy is trying to determine if we have any more burials in the immediate area. We're in the middle of a small barrow."

"I'd rather stay with you."

"Okay." Handing him a small trowel and a brush, Davida watched him follow her to the ground. "Then you can help me liberate Stanley here."

She showed Jensen how to carefully clear the soil from around the bones before leaning back to watch him work with the same meticulous concentration he studied contracts. As hard as it was to accept, her absence and her accomplishments had changed him in ways she'd never believed possible. While she resented that such extreme measures were necessary to facilitate the change, she understood where he was coming from back in the day.

She'd been a bright-eyed grad student chasing big dreams when they met. Love had tempered those ambitions by the time they married. She'd already decided to put her dreams on hold and imitate her mother by the time she walked down the aisle. To stay close to home instead of venturing off to excavate exotic cultures as she'd always planned. Her new life and husband meant more than the glorious career she'd always wanted. Jensen knew that, and he'd acted accordingly.

Mentally shaking her head at her naivete, Davida mourned the loss of that youthful innocence. She'd been so idealistic compared to the socialites Jensen dated. With maturity, she now understood why he'd doubted her convictions. She'd doubted them herself.

To quote Dan, she'd been refreshing in her exuberance. Right. She'd wanted to be refreshing almost as much as she wanted to be nice. Both terms were as exciting as plain spaghetti without butter or salt. Forget the marinara.

However, he was right. She'd made no secret that she wanted a life with Jensen. Nor had she hidden the fact that she expected to have that life on her terms. Surprisingly, Jensen agreed. He'd tolerate finishing her MA before their real lives started. She'd found that compromise acceptable, believing that when her degree was in hand, she'd be ready to move on to the next phase of their marriage. Nothing could be further from the truth.

While Jensen believed she'd be content with her philanthropic endeavors and raising two or three little Blakes, in her heart, she knew differently. The last thing she'd wanted in the first few years of marriage was to get pregnant. Not that she wouldn't love her children, she would. Desperately. But the thought of motherhood scared her witless.

However, she'd promised to give her husband the family he wanted, and Jensen believed her. He had no reason not to. He'd seen the same scenario play out with his mother. Tara gave up a promising legal career to raise her family in a time when there weren't that many female attorneys out there. Just getting through school and passing the bar exam was a major accomplishment. That she'd been a prominent attorney at a large, well-established Atlanta firm before her marriage was staggering.

From what Davida could see, she'd channeled her brilliance and energy into her charities and maintaining the family image in the years since she gave up her legal practice. Tara excelled at both and found contentment in a job well done. While her mother-in-law was happy with her sacrifice, it didn't take long to realize she wouldn't be. She'd wanted more.

"What has you so deep in thought?" Jensen's voice penetrated her contemplation. "You haven't said a word in close to two hours."

She'd been too focused on carefully picking pieces of metal and wood from the dirt.

"You," Davida admitted. "And the fact I never thought I'd see this day."

"Neither did I," Jensen agreed. "But things have changed. I think you're starting to see that now."

He'd changed. More than she thought possible. The old him wouldn't have respected her ignoring him in favor of her work. However, the man he was now felt different. He'd watched her carefully expose Stanley bit by bit and followed suit. It hadn't taken long to get as immersed in his assignment as she was. He'd been surprised that hours had passed when he finally sat back to interrupt her concentration.

"I think I am." She smiled at the tender way Jensen brushed dirt from Stanley's lower arm. "We think Stan here might be royalty. A high-ranking aristocrat at the least and a seasoned warrior either way."

"How do you know that?" Catching a faint glint of metal, Jensen brushed dirt from his hand. "I just see bones and fabric."

"We're fortunate the skeleton is mostly intact." Davida sat back on her haunches. "A lot of times we lose most or all the bones to acidic soil. That didn't happen this time, so I'm reasonably confident Stan's a young male from the size and shape of his pelvis. There's a chance that I'm wrong. If I'm right, he was roughly 15 to 25 when he died, with enough previously healed injuries on his bones to confirm he knew how to wield that second sword that's still half buried by your left foot. As for his cause of death, he died from a weapon that cleaved his skull. Probably a sword."

"How do you know that?" Jensen repeated. "The damage to his skull could have happened postmortem."

He'd watched enough late-night forensic shows to know that it was possible if they were to be believed.

"Because I know what I'm looking at." Between taking the right classes and her field work, she had an impressive arsenal of knowledge in her head. "See this?" She reached out to touch a spot on the skull. "Stan lived long enough for the bone to begin healing. See these holes here and here, and how the bone has thickened around the injury? He developed a bone infection that eventually killed him."

She spoke with the absolute confidence of experience. This wasn't her first case of osteomyelitis. It wouldn't be her last.

"Is this what you do all the time?" Jensen continued freeing the crest of a ring from the soil. "It's not quite what I imagined."

"Not necessarily," Davida admitted. "I don't always have a Stanley. Sometimes it's just post holes or pottery shards. Just ordinary, everyday pieces to a bigger puzzle we're trying to put together. When I'm not out here," she turned in the direction of their workstation. "I might be over there taking care of paperwork related to the dig. I'll try to let you see how everything works before you go. Right now, we need to get that ring documented."

"From what I've uncovered so far, it looks like filigreed gold with a large center garnet."

"Filigreed gold with a large center garnet?" Davida cocked her head. "Excuse me, when did you become an expert on Dark Age jewelry?"

"I may have looked up Anglo-Saxon artifacts on the plane ride over." Jensen made a sheepish face. "I may have even read a little bit about a bed burial or two, not knowing that was what you'd found. It was interesting."

"I see." Davida laughed softly. "You were reading about dead people when you should have been studying contracts."

"I'd already finished with the contracts," Jensen admitted. "I needed something to occupy my time."

"That sounds more like the man I know." Davida sat on the side of the trench. "Have you checked in yet?"

There were several nice hotels in the surrounding towns. No doubt he'd picked the best of the lot. While not extravagant, Jensen had upgraded from his youthful bed and a coffeemaker mentality to something more executive class. His job was stressful. Having a comfortable place to unwind after a long day was a necessary expense.

"I don't have a reservation anywhere." He had a first cousin twice removed that he could impose on if necessary. "I wanted to see you first."

Okay. She could accept that. However, the truth was closer to the fact that, if things didn't go well at their meeting, there wouldn't be any reason to stay. They both knew that. However, the chance of that happening at this point was slim to none.

"Tom's parents may have a vacancy at their place." Davida volunteered. "It's a nice, upscale inn around the corner from the Trousered Viking. I can set you up with a room, or you could stay at my place if you like."

"Are you ready for that?"

"I invited you to my house." Davida's tone was serious. "Not my bed." She had two free bedrooms and a sleeper sofa if it came to that.

"Don't you think that's tempting fate?" Jensen stared her down.

"Maybe," Davida answered honestly. "But I'll take my chances if you will."

Whatever happened would happen. It wasn't like she hadn't already burned her bridges with Tom or committed to a different course. The only question was when, and they'd both agreed to let that happen naturally. If organic were sooner rather than later, so be it. She could live with that.

"I will."

"Then I'll take you to my place when we finish." Davida rose to her feet. "You can settle in while I come back here to wrap things up for the night. The team usually meets at the pub to grab a bite before we all head home. We don't have to go if you don't want to, but I think you'd enjoy yourself. What do you say?"

"We go." Jensen nodded. "It's been a while since I've had pub food."

"Okay." Davida nodded. "Then I'll let Leslie know we're leaving for a while. I'll swing by the house when I'm done. We can walk to the pub together."

"Sounds good," Jensen agreed. "I'll settle in and check in with the office to make sure there isn't anything I need to deal with. After that, I'm free."

"You won't regret it." Davida motioned for him to follow her. "Hey, Leslie, I'm going to take Jensen to the house, then I'll come back and help you lock down."

"You want me to finish recording that ring while you're gone?" Leslie grabbed a ruler and a camera at her nod. "I'll let everyone know we're done for the day. Usual time and place?"

"Yep." Davida dusted her hands on her jeans. "Nothing has changed."

"Everything's changed, and you're so in for it." Leslie laughed at Davida's expression. "Hey, we're nosey. We wouldn't do this for a living if we weren't."

"Whatever." Davida rolled her eyes as she grabbed Jensen's arm. "Let's get out of here before that one gets in more trouble than she already is."

Watching them leave, Leslie laughed before she headed in the opposite direction. Like it or not, her boss knew she was right. If there was one thing the locals thrived on, it was gossip. If Davida thought being American exempted her from wagging tongues, she had another think coming. She'd been adopted a long time ago.

CHAPTER TWENTY

"**I**'m so glad that's over!" Davida tossed her purse on a table in passing before collapsing on the couch. "I thought they'd never stop giving me the third degree. Leslie was the worst."

"Did you expect anything different?" Jensen pushed his teacup in her direction, confident she wouldn't mind him making use of her well-stocked cupboards. "While it wasn't my intent, my appearance stirred things up."

"It did." Davida took a sip of tea from his cup. "Man, that's good. When did you start drinking tea?"

She meant hot, not iced, and they both knew it.

"I was about five when my grandmother introduced me to afternoon tea." Davida smiled at the mental picture. "That included how to make a proper cup."

"That still doesn't explain why I've only seen you drink iced tea before now." The fact that she was a coffee drinker may have played a part in that. "I thought I knew your preferences."

"You do." Jensen agreed. "When I'm stateside. When I travel, I tend to have a when in Rome attitude. It makes life a whole lot easier to just go with the flow. There's no reason you would know that."

Unlike Sharon, they hadn't traveled much together. Not internationally. Not unless you counted their honeymoon to Greece and Italy, when a good cup of tea was the last thing on his mind.

"No, there isn't." Davida agreed, knowing that would change now. "We're meeting everyone in less than an hour, so

I need to change. We'll take the scenic route rather than the straight shot through town."

"I'm assuming that will take longer."

"Some." Davida rose to her feet. "We're meeting later because it took longer to get everything shut down." Largely because of all the annoying questions.

"I'm assuming you guys usually go straight from work."

"Usually, but tonight's special," Davida admitted. "You're here, and it's our first real date in five years."

"I hadn't thought about that." He just wanted to see her. "Although it's more like a group date."

"I guess it is." Davida leaned over to kiss his cheek. "But it's still a date."

Laughing at her sassy take it or leave it tone, Jensen resisted the urge to follow her. There would be time for that later. For now, they had places to go and people to meet. Draining his cup, he ambled into the kitchen, washed the cup, and put it away.

Returning to the den, he popped off a few text messages and read the responses. Hearing steps on the stairs, he checked his watch before putting it away. It had taken Davi all of twenty minutes to shower and change.

"You ready?" Davida entered the room. "Let me get our coats so we can go."

Turning at the sound of her voice, Jensen took a moment to drink in her appearance. There was a casual elegance about the crimson cashmere sweater and black dress slacks that showed off her svelte figure, which was different from what she used to wear. More sophisticated and less girlish. The unexpected touch of gold on the heels of her comfortable booties, chunkier gold jewelry, and brighter makeup hinted at changes in her personality he'd never seen. There was an assertive confidence about her that her younger self didn't have.

"You look beautiful." Jensen held her coat for her to slide into. "You smell good, too."

She still wore the same light, woodsy scent he remembered from so long ago.

"It's the body wash your mom brought me from London the last Christmas we were all together." They'd been married about eighteen months at the time. "I found the shop she used soon after I moved here. It's a custom perfumery that's been in business for over three hundred years, but I bet you already know that."

"I didn't." He didn't know a lot about his mother's haunts. "Mom went to law school in London, so she knows the shops much better than I ever will."

"I guess she does." Davida opened the door. "We need to go if we don't want to be late." She looped her arm through his. "You know my team's going to give us hell."

"They can try." He wasn't worried in the least. "If we can handle bulldozer Barb, we can handle the peanut gallery."

"I guess we can." Davida pointed out the 11th-century pre-conquest church in passing. "I'm nervous about you meeting Tom."

"Why?" Jensen stopped to look at her. "I thought he was dating Leslie."

"He is," Davida confirmed. "Don't you think it's going to be awkward?"

"For a little while." Jensen agreed. "We'll get through it."

From her expression, Davida wasn't as sure.

"Look, you both knew something wasn't right, so the breakup was inevitable." She wouldn't go that far, but Jensen was entitled to his opinion. "I honestly think your ex and I are more interested in sizing each other up than causing you grief. Once we get past the male posturing, we'll get along fine."

"I'll take your word for it." Davida sounded dubious. "And I'll try not to laugh if you're right."

"Then we need to get in there." Jensen nodded in the direction of the building on the next block. "How old is that place?"

Seriously old by the looks of it.

"The main part is tenth century or older." The earliest records date to 945, but other sources hint that the building went back to the reign of Eanred. "The older addition was built in the 13th century, soon after Tom's family bought the building and expanded the pub. The newest addition was built in the 16th century as the business grew."

Jensen added that tidbit to what he already knew about her ex. He'd asked a friend to do some discreet digging soon after learning the other man existed. Like any man in a similar situation, he'd wanted to size up the competition. It hadn't taken much to discover Tom's last name. From there, the rest was easy.

He now knew his name, age, and what he looked like. He'd received a couple of photos he hadn't paid much attention to. Handsome was a low requirement on his wife's priority list. There were other characteristics she valued more, like intelligence, stability, faithfulness, and family orientation. All characteristics that Thomas seemed to possess in abundance. He hadn't liked discovering that.

There were a lot of things he hadn't enjoyed learning about the other man. Things like Tom owned a nice house in the village and the pub outright. He'd inherited both from his grandfather soon after he completed university. Inherited and immediately went to work to ensure he made his family proud.

An only child, he'd inherit the rest of the business when his parents died. Looking over the available records, the businesses were doing well and always had been. The family's long history of working hard and living beneath their means allowed them to weather unavoidable storms. He wasn't surprised by that. Blake had survived in much the same way.

While Davida couldn't care less about power, money, or position, she wouldn't tie herself to an irresponsible man. She'd worked too hard to get where she was to lose her reputation over a partner's actions. Thinking back, Jensen silently acknowledged that while he hadn't been happy to discover Tom was financially secure, he was pleased Davida would have a comfortable life if he lost his gamble.

"Interesting." Jensen opened the door and ushered her inside. "I take it the blonde gentleman with his arm around Leslie is Tom."

He knew it was. He'd studied the photographs in his file enough to recognize the other man. He'd also noticed the photographs still dotting his wife's home. There was nothing subtle about her message. She was letting him know they weren't a done deal yet.

She might have burned her bridges with Tom, but there were other fish in the sea if he failed to seal the deal. They were out there, and she wasn't averse to finding them now that he'd had his second chance. Right. That wasn't happening on his watch. The woman was his, whether she wanted to accept it or not. Just as he was hers. That never changed in the five years she was gone.

"You take it right." Davida led the way towards the back of the room with Jensen in tow. "Hey, everyone, long time, no see."

Ignoring the expected titters, Jensen felt the air suck out of the room as he and Tom openly sized each other up. Like it or not, the other man was good-looking if you dug the tall, athletic, blonde, British actor look. Fortunately, Davida leaned towards the even taller, dark American magnate look more.

"Hello, Tom." Deciding to let Davida off the hook for the introductions, Jensen offered his hand. "It's nice to finally meet you."

"Same here." Tom shook his hand, firmly accepting the silent challenge. "Davi said you were coming when she dropped by earlier."

Davida made a face at the raised brow. So, she'd stopped by on her way home after closing the site. While she knew Leslie would alert Tom to Jensen's early arrival, she'd needed to soften the blow. She owed him that much.

"My business in London finished earlier than expected." Jensen felt the tension leave the air as he pulled a chair out for his wife. "I decided to take advantage of the extra time to surprise Davi."

Exchanging small talk, Jensen accompanied Tom to the bar to grab a couple of sodas. Glancing at the menu, he placed an order for a couple of fish sandwiches complete with chips. He'd come back to pick up their baskets when they were ready. For now, he was going to enjoy spending time with his wife and her nutty friends.

"...Then the ram butted the skull over the wall like a football." Taking his seat by Davida, Jensen caught the tail end of Brad's tale. "No, I didn't goal kick it back over the wall. The skull, nor the sheep." The brunette asking the question was Ansley, if he remembered right. "I had to make like a snake and slide down the hill to fetch the bloody thing, then climb back up again."

"Hadrian's wall," Davida whispered. "Brad was startled by a huge sheep on a dig. The ram had issues with the Roman skull he'd just uncovered."

Or, more likely, with Brad digging on his turf.

"I see." Jensen wondered briefly if this was what archaeologists did for fun and decided it wasn't that bad, seeing the smiling faces around him. "Sounds traumatizing."

"It was." Brad agreed. "I was rather glad he went for the skull. It gave me time to get out of the way before he did any permanent damage."

Shaking his head at the ridiculous picture in his mind, Jensen rose to fetch their meal. Even across the room, he could hear Toby recounting the discovery of a skeleton that turned out to be a taller female gladiator from some mainland tribe. Sliding into the seat beside her, Jensen handed Davida her basket, smiling at the rapture on her face. For someone so small, the girl could eat.

Accepting her basket, Davida smiled her thanks before turning back to Toby. No matter how many times she heard stories from the field, they never got old. She was thrilled when another piece of the puzzle clicked into place, and it showed.

Just listening to her assistant go through each revelation gave her tangible goose bumps. The gladiatrix's DNA revealed Pulcheria came from somewhere near modern-day Belgium. Her reconstructed headstone proudly declared she'd earned her freedom through gladiatorial contests, and she was the "beloved wife" of Gaius. Her bones betrayed she'd died somewhere around age forty. If that wasn't enough, the quality of her elaborately carved coffin and grave goods indicated her husband was prosperous.

"From other headstones we found, almost everyone in that part of the cemetery died from some plague." Toby took a moment to reflect on the loss. "Probably measles or smallpox since she died around the time of the Antonine Plague."

"I'm assuming you did the facial reconstruction?"

"Oh, yeah." Toby was a forensic artist long before he became an archaeologist. "Our girl was a striking blue-eyed blonde you'd look at twice if you saw her walking down a Brussels street."

"Oh, shoot." Davida pushed her empty basket aside. "You were with Dr. K's dig back in 2015."

She should have connected the dots before now. Katie Atwood was something of a legend in her book. She'd uncovered a vast necropolis back in the day, complete with one of the handful of female gladiators ever found.

Most memorable about that find was that Pulcheria's profession was never in doubt. It was carved on her headstone. In words and images. Davida remembered how enamored she'd been with that whole discovery. Especially the facial reconstruction.

"She was a real head turner in several ways." Davida continued. "While your reconstruction was breathtaking, that woman was several inches taller than most men of the day."

"She was taller than her husband." Toby agreed. "And at least twenty years younger. Dr. Atwood found Gaius' grave in a different part of the necropolis a couple of years later."

Davida hadn't known that. She'd abandoned outside interests once her plate was filled with graduate studies and marriage. That was a real shame. She'd missed out on a lot.

Becoming aware of how long she'd ignored her guest, she turned to look at Jensen. From his expression, he was enjoying himself as much as she was, which surprised her. That impression was reinforced by the gentle pressure of his hand against hers beneath the table.

"Why was he buried in a different part of the cemetery than his wife?" That didn't make sense. "I'm assuming that part filled up before he died?"

"That's what Katie believed." Toby agreed. "Or maybe anyone who knew where his wife was buried was gone by then."

While a sad thought, that was a definite possibility. Whole communities were often wiped out by plagues or decimated to the point that they never recovered. That may have happened in this instance. It wouldn't surprise her.

"This is fascinating." Davida leaned back in her chair. "I don't know how I missed the connection on your resume."

"Why wouldn't you?" He was already part of the team when she arrived. "I can't wait to give Stanley a face."

Davida laughed softly at his enthusiasm. She didn't have to say anything. Toby knew their hands were tied until that section of the grid was done and the finds were fully documented. He couldn't risk another sneaky, unauthorized labor of love.

"Enough with the shop talk." Leslie threw a limp chip at Davida. "Tamsyn called a couple of days ago. She just married some celebrity chef she met in Grasse three days ago."

"Yeah, well, she's a wild child, so I'm not surprised by that." Davida's calm demeanor indicated she wasn't shocked at all. "Why didn't she call me?"

"Why do you think?" Leslie laughed in her pint. "Who would you call? The chick making randy comments about the hottie you snagged and his prowess in bed, or the one asking if you've finally flipped your lid?"

"Only you, my friend, only you."

Leslie was a bit of a wild child herself.

"I rest my case."

Turning to Jensen, Davida briefly explained that Tamsyn was the third member of their all-girls club. The insane one. Literally. This latest stunt proved it. Quirking a brow, she couldn't believe her husband was laughing at her. Or that he was siding with the enemy. Huffing, she turned back to Leslie to get the rest of the story.

"They're taking a culinary tour of the Mediterranean before they settle down at his parents' winery in Napa Valley."

Davida couldn't help laughing at how preposterous the whole thing sounded. Tami's perky, bespectacled cuteness belied her uninhibited, quirky personality. On the surface, she looked like the librarian she was. A super cute, faintly sexy bibliosoph, but still a librarian. Under the surface, she was anything but.

"Okay." The story kept getting better. "I hope she plans on swinging by Cornwall to let her parents know she's not in London anymore."

Rolling her eyes, Leslie threw another chip at her boss and changed the subject. Tamsyn was their resident free spirit. She should be cheering her on! It wasn't like either of them would ever bop over to France as a single working girl and return a few days later as a married woman.

Then again, maybe one of them just had. Davi had bopped across the pond to reunite with the ghost of a bygone era, and what a ghost he was. Doable without the dough, in her opinion. Irresistible with it. Besides, anyone with one eye and half a brain could see the woman was still head over heels in love with the man, whether she knew it or not.

No wonder she'd kicked Tom to the curb. Not that Leslie wasn't grateful. She was. She'd wanted that man long before he dated her boss. Unfortunately, they'd been dating other people when they met. When they finally weren't, they'd both been too badly burned to act on any attraction. About the time they were ready to move on, Davi appeared, and the rest was history.

Not that she'd mourned the missed opportunity. She hadn't. She'd moved on, too, and dated an old school chum for a while. She'd had a blast while it lasted. Neither she nor Jeremy was in it for the long haul, and they both knew it. But they enjoyed each other's company. Who wouldn't enjoy dating a free-wheeling barrister with more money than sense? Added to that, he was great in the sack.

In the interim, she and Tom had become good friends. How could they not? He was friends with everyone on the dig. They were in his pub almost every night. While strictly platonic, they'd both recognized the sizzle under the surface and chose not to pursue it.

However, that didn't mean they didn't know it was there. That awareness allowed them to tumble into bed within minutes of Tom admitting Davi cut him loose. The experience was everything they expected, and he hadn't slept in his bed since. She wouldn't let him if he tried.

Leslie laughed softly. Tom now had more clothes hanging in her closet than she did. Not that she was complaining. She was perfectly content with the way things were. Watching Davi with Jensen tonight eased her conscience over how quickly she'd jumped her best friend's ex.

The truth was, she'd moved so fast because she didn't want another woman to get her paws on her man. That had already happened once. She didn't want it to happen again. However, her actions weren't without consequence. Like how awkward she'd felt the next day at work when she'd confessed what they'd done.

Fortunately, Davida was glad Tom moved on. There was no denying she felt guilty about what happened in Atlanta. It didn't matter that she'd always been honest about her situation. If she'd had any issues with how quickly their hook-up occurred, she kept them to herself. All she'd asked was that they be discreet until everyone got used to the idea that she and Tom weren't together anymore. That no one had done anything wrong on either side. That she was fine with him being with Leslie. Why wouldn't she be when she'd walked away first?

They'd done as she asked, and everything fell into place. Neither the dig nor the close camaraderie of the team was disrupted. Davi had expertly defused a situation that could have turned ugly fast. Instead, everyone now understood that not only had she reconciled with her husband, but Tom and Leslie had her blessing. Looking around the table, she caught her boss's eye and lifted her pint in silent approval. Any way you cut it, the man by her side was a keeper.

CHAPTER TWENTY-ONE

L aughing at Jensen's running commentary on her team's high jinks throughout the evening, Davida struggled to insert her key in the lock. Pulling her hand from her husband's grip, she finally got the job done.

"Would you stop?" Getting a hold of herself, Davida pushed the door open and stepped inside. "Here, I had this made for you so you can come and go as you please."

She took a key out of her purse and gave it to him. Closing the door, she watched Jensen put the key on his ring. He didn't say anything, but she could see he was pleased by the gesture. While it wasn't a guarantee, that she was willing to go this far was a good omen.

"It's a safe bet Leslie won't be dropping by tonight, so we don't have to worry about interruptions."

"I think you're right."

From what he'd seen, Leslie was far more likely to drop by Tom's place for a sleepover than Davida's for work.

"I know it." Davida laughed softly as he followed her into the den. "I'll meet you in here in a few. Right now, I'm going to change into something more comfortable."

Watching Davida disappear around the corner with their coats in hand, Jensen studied the room in a way he hadn't earlier. While it was true he'd made a cup of tea in her kitchen, he hadn't taken the time to study his surroundings.

He'd dissected every moment he'd worked side-by-side with his wife at her dig instead. Discovering that ring was exciting. He hadn't expected to uncover anything but finger bones.

Looking around him now, he understood why Davi loved this place so much. It was homey and historical. The two H's she loved best.

He was more impressed that the modernizations hadn't damaged the historic integrity in any way than he was with the house itself. While a solid build, the updates were recent and professionally done. That was good. The more he looked, the more he liked the house. He liked the whole village. Ashworth was a beautiful throwback to a bygone era.

If things played out the way he hoped, he might buy this place. He would certainly make a few calls before he left the U.K. He might even make an offer. The idea made sense on several fronts. First, Davida would get a comfortable home base for the next few years. Second, he'd have a peaceful getaway in a beautiful setting. The third, the house appeared structurally sound with no repairs or updates necessary. There wasn't a downside to any of that. He'd analyze the financial feasibility later.

Right now, his interests were better served by devoting his attention to his wife than to future endeavors. Settling on the couch, Jensen watched Davida return to take her place beside him. He wasn't surprised she wore a well-worn night shirt that skimmed her thighs and no slippers. It seemed some things never changed. Not that she needed anything more. Her home was comfortably warm compared to the outside temperature.

"I'm sorry that I never asked how your meetings went." She leaned back against a pillow and automatically placed her bare feet on his lap without asking. "I haven't even thought about your work before tonight."

Jensen watched her eyes drift shut as he applied pressure to the sole of her foot. Shaking his head, he was surprised Davida still had no clue how appealing she was. It didn't hurt that she wore next to nothing beneath her favorite sleep shirt. While he'd caught a flash of dark lace when his wife plopped on the couch, it was obvious she'd jettisoned the matching bra somewhere along the way.

"You haven't had time." Pulling his mind from the gutter, Jensen concentrated on her foot, noting she still wore the same bright red nail polish she used to wear. "You were too busy getting inundated with discoveries."

From what he remembered of the wildly chaotic day he'd just

spent, it seemed they were uncovering another artifact every few minutes.

"To answer your question, my meetings went well. The complex in London is filled with long-term tenants, and the shops are thriving. Dad will be happy that the renovations have finally paid off."

No, his mother would be thrilled since she'd inherited their U.K. holdings from her grandmother. Technically, she owned the properties even if she'd left managing them in her husband's capable hands. Now, those responsibilities fell to him. Not only did he have to ensure his father's company was profitable, but his mother's holdings as well. The upside was that he made frequent trips to the U.K.

"I'm glad." Davida smiled as Jensen massaged her bare foot. "I'd forgotten how well you do that."

"You wound me." Setting her right foot back on his lap, Jensen switched his ministrations to her left. "My many talents are unforgettable."

Ignoring his salacious tone, Davina flexed her foot as a kink dissolved beneath his fingers. She couldn't deny how content they'd once been. Happy. Even when they were mind-numbingly busy, they'd always found time to steal loving moments like this amid chaos.

With time and distance, it was beyond her how she ever believed Jensen cheated on her. Especially with that despicable, manipulative sneak. She'd never had any reason to distrust him. He'd gone out of his way to ensure she didn't. For a wealthy businessman, Jensen was surprisingly transparent with her.

She'd always known his schedule and how to contact him when he was out of town. Added to that, he'd never dismissed one of her calls, even when he was in a meeting. Then again, she'd never knowingly called when he was actively conducting business.

"All better." Rolling to a sitting position, Davida rose to her feet. "Thank you."

"You're welcome." Jensen followed her towards the kitchen. "Why don't we open the champagne I brought? We have a lot to celebrate."

Like her discoveries and their reconciliation.

"I suppose we do." Davida turned to face him. "I'll get the glasses. You pop the cork."

Reaching towards a cabinet, she found herself pulled back against Jensen instead. Closing her eyes, she leaned against him, savoring the scent of his cologne. Feeling him turn her around, she wasn't all that surprised to feel his lips against hers before strong hands lifted her to sit on the countertop. The look on her husband's face told Davida she wouldn't be pouring wine anytime soon. He'd waited long enough.

"I think we've visited here recently."

Wrapping her legs around his waist, Davida was surprised by how ready she was to feel his weight pressing into her.

"Yeah?" Reaching beneath her sleep shirt, he made short work of removing the minuscule barrier between them. "Maybe not."

Davida gasped at his sudden invasion, wondering how she'd ever forgotten this all-consuming possession. Moaning softly, she pulled his shirt over his head before running her palms over his chest. It didn't seem possible he was in better shape than when she'd left, but he was. Then again, so was she. However, there was no denying Jensen felt good. Too good. On too many levels.

Hanging on for dear life, she returned every decadent thrust, ignoring the memories flooding her mind. Recalling all the places and ways they'd been together didn't serve any real purpose beyond winding her up. Right now, the emotions his touch evoked were more intense than she could process. She'd settle for mindless sex instead. Closing her eyes, she gave in to sensation, quickly falling apart in his arms.

The shuddering of his body beneath her palms and the press of his forehead against hers betrayed their mutual completion in a way word and sound never could. Gently lowering her legs, Jensen straightened her gown and refastened his pants. He'd grab his shirt from the floor in a minute.

"I won't apologize for something I don't regret." He rested his palms against her waist. "Or for one of the best experiences of my life."

Piercing her with his gaze, he shook his head, thinking that opinion had nothing to do with the physical act as mutually satisfying as it was, but with the knowledge she'd freely given herself without reservation.

"Then I won't ask you to." Davida brushed her lips against his as she slid off the counter. "It takes two to tango, and I didn't say no."

Pulling away, she turned to the cabinet, aware that her husband was shadowing her like a hungry puppy. Removing two flutes and setting them aside, Davida popped the cork on the champagne.

"It's been a few years since I've had this." She noted it was a demi of the expensive wine they'd shared at their wedding reception. "I think I drank more in those few days we were together than I have in the last couple of years."

Jensen nodded as he buttoned his shirt and cleaned up. Davida was never much for drinking, although she was infamous for stealing a sip or two from his glass when the mood struck. It was interesting she'd stayed such a lightweight considering she spent most nights at the pub with Tom and her team. Then again, alcohol made her sleepy. Because of that, she'd rather have a coffee or a cup of tea than a glass of wine or a pint any day.

"So, you're flying to Edinburgh on the day after tomorrow?" Davida tentatively took a sip and set her glass aside. "I'd forgotten how good that is."

"Your favorite," Jensen reminded her, carrying both of their glasses back to the couch. "I'm flying to Edinburgh on Wednesday morning. I'll be in meetings for two or three days, then I'm flying home. I'll be up to my eyeballs in contracts for the next month or so, ironing out a new deal. After that, things are pretty normal for a while."

Normal was still insanely busy. She already knew that. However, Jensen was letting her know she probably wouldn't see him for five or six weeks. The honeymoon was over. Real life was leeching in.

"Okay, well, you know what's going on here." Davida referenced his recent visit to the site. "It'll get crazy for a while. Bed burials are big deals. If I'm right and our warrior is male, that's an even bigger deal. Male burials of this type are extremely rare in the UK. All but one or two are women. Most of them are Christian. Our guy isn't. Not from what we've uncovered so far. Or he may be straddling both fences. Either way, I have people to update, a grid to rework, and weeks of paperwork to wade through."

Just thinking about what had happened since her return was mind-boggling. Both at the site and here.

"At this point, I can't say when I'll be back in Georgia. Just that the end of the season will be later than expected. I can't abandon my commitments because we've reconciled."

While it wouldn't change anything, she hoped he'd accept the ugly truth without a fight. Hopefully, after this visit, he finally understood how important her work was.

"No, you can't." He didn't like it, but he wouldn't ask her to wreck the career she'd worked so hard to establish. Not anymore. As hard as it was to admit, he would have done just that in the past. "However, that doesn't mean I can't fly over every few weeks to spend time together. Who knows, that may work out better for us in the long run."

They would have the opportunity to nurture their relationship without the pressures of being thrust together 24/7. He wasn't sure how that would work out. They were still in the infancy of rebuilding their life together. He wasn't under any illusion that sex was a magic pill that made everything all right. If anything, it complicated matters.

"It may." Davida set her glass aside. "As reluctant as I was in the beginning, things are falling into place quicker than I expected."

"Then you're not against my plan." He'd expected more resistance. "I'll check my schedule when I get back and let you know when I can come over. We'll figure out the specifics then."

"Sounds good." Davida took a sip of champagne. "If I'm not here working on notes or down at the site, you'll find me at the Viking, squirreled away in our corner. In the meantime, come and go as you please. You have a key."

"Or I could just call you." Jensen quirked a brow at her. "Ask where you are and let you know I'm coming."

Davida snorted.

"Good luck with that." She grabbed her cell. "You know how well this thing works out in the field."

"I guess I do." He agreed. "Then I'll take my chances and track you down."

"You do that." Davida laughed at the look on his face. "Right now, you can start marking your territory by moving your things into my room. At this point, having separate bedrooms is ridiculous, don't you think?"

"Unless you regret what happened." Jensen's tone was quiet. "I don't."

"Not yet." She leaned a little closer. "You should probably know I'm not on anything, and the thought of turning you down didn't cross my mind."

"That's not like you." Past tragedies aside, they'd had a timeline in mind for starting their family, and they'd stuck to it. He'd expected the same forethought and responsibility this time around. "I took it for granted you were."

She always had been, including on that fateful getaway. Perhaps they would have realized the truth in time if she hadn't been. For an unknown reason, her pill failed miserably.

"I wasn't because I didn't think I was ready. Then I realized it didn't matter." Davida straddled his lap and took his face in her hands. "I said yes, so whatever happens, I'm okay with it."

"So am I," Jensen admitted. "You should probably know Dan revoked his threat now that we're back together. While he'd prefer to see his grandchild before he dies, he isn't forcing the issue anymore."

"While that's good to know, I'm not with you because of some silly threat." Davida pulled her nightshirt over her head as she felt Jensen harden at the sight of her naked body. "You already know that."

Pressing her lips to his, she wasn't surprised to feel strong fingers reverently brush rapidly puckering nipples.

"I do." Reaching up to flick her hair out of her eyes, Jensen's fingers followed the curve of Davida's cheek and neck before dropping to cup her right breast while his other hand rested lightly on her hip to offer stability. "Once you calm down and think things through, you don't do anything you don't want to. I wouldn't be here if this wasn't what you want, and you certainly wouldn't be straddling my lap, unbuttoning my shirt in that take-charge manner."

"You're right." Davida reached for his belt. "I don't, and I wouldn't be. But I had to reach that conclusion for myself."

She had to finally accept that she never wanted to leave in the first place. She'd felt compelled to. About the time she'd decided to fight for her marriage, no matter how it looked, all hell broke loose. She'd reacted instead of acted, and it cost her marriage. Now that she was on the precipice of reclaiming everything she thought she'd lost, she refused to repeat past mistakes. It wasn't a sin to admit she wanted to save her marriage or that she wanted this.

"I guess you did." Jensen kicked off his pants and leaned back against the couch, secretly enjoying the feel of her heat rubbing torturously against his hardness. "Why don't you tell me what's on the agenda for tomorrow?"

Tamping down on the desire to buck inside her teasing folds, Jensen decided to let Davi have her fun instead.

"I cleared my schedule," Davida smirked at the open surprise on his face. "Tomorrow is a housekeeping day when we clean artifacts and make sure all our records are up to date and in order. The team doesn't need me for that. They'll probably prefer not having me around, cracking the whip, the slackers. We'll all meet at the pub around seven if that's okay with you."

None of her team were slackers, and they didn't need her looking over their shoulders while they completed routine paperwork. Nor did they need her to supervise cleaning artifacts.

She had three well-trained conservators who did the detail work. She could afford to take the rare day off, even if it meant they'd get ribbed mercilessly at the pub.

"Sounds good." Jensen closed his eyes and moaned as Davida engulfed him with a roll of her hips that almost undid both of them. "Stop. If you do that again, neither of us is going to be very happy."

Halting, Davida savored how perfectly they fit together as she waited for Jensen to compose himself. Closing her eyes, she smiled when the hands lightly gripping her hips suddenly urged her into a familiar rhythm her body still knew. How could she ever forget how good this felt?

Feeling Jensen shift, she allowed him to lie her back on the couch and cover her body with his. Lifting her arms over her head, she met him thrust for thrust, knowing this wasn't a repeat of their earlier session. While neither of them was averse to the occasional quickie, they both preferred leisurely loving to chasing an orgasm. From the way Jensen was nuzzling her neck, she was in for a long night of sensual adoration that she intended to return touch for intimate touch.

CHAPTER TWENTY-TWO

S taring around the room, Davida tapped her fingers on the edge of the exam table. Even knowing Karen would be with her as soon as possible, wallowing in apprehension was growing old fast. The fact that the other woman was a close friend, as well as her doctor, didn't make the not knowing any easier. If she didn't get in here soon, she'd go looking for her.

It was one thing to come in for her required yearly physical. It was another thing entirely to get called back to the doctor's surgery when her labs came in. Whatever they'd found in her bloodwork concerned Karen enough to request a consultation. While probably nothing serious since the visit was scheduled at her convenience, she still didn't like knowing something was off.

Not when she was so busy. Not when she'd been right about that grave. It was a bed burial, and it was male. Not only male, but likely a continental pagan princeling as well. The trustees were ecstatic, and the press was a pain in her rear. They'd had to employ extra security to keep the casual gawkers out.

As much as she had on her plate right now, there wasn't time to be sick. She wasn't sick. She felt great. Maybe a little anemic. That would make sense. If she thought about it, she was tired by the end of the day. More than tired. Exhausted. That was a little unusual. She didn't normally need more than four or five hours of sleep a night to be fully rested. Both of her parents were like that.

"You look better than you did a few days ago." Karen walked into the room with a file in her hand. "Things must have calmed down at the site."

"Some." Davida agreed. "Enough to get more sleep."

"That's good." The dark-haired woman sat on a stool and put her file aside. "Ah, you weren't wearing those last time I saw you."

She nodded at the rings on Davida's left hand.

"No, I wasn't." Davida agreed. "I don't wear much jewelry in the field, and I came straight from the site that day. I had meetings in York today, so I decided to dress up a little."

It was the first time she'd had her wedding rings in place since Jensen left. It wasn't practical to wear them in the trenches. She needed to talk to her husband about getting a plain gold band to wear on a chain around her neck when it wasn't on her finger. There was something comforting about that idea while they were so far apart.

"I'm assuming you didn't marry Tom since the whole village knows he's cozied up with Leslie now," Karen quirked a brow. "So, you either have some unknown hottie hiding in the wings or you're back with the missing husband."

"The hubby," Davida admitted. "Jensen and I reconciled when I went home to see my dad. He visited me here while you were in Wales."

Karen had been buried in work since her return, or she would have heard the village gossip. It was clear she hadn't. That said volumes about how far behind the eight ball the woman was. That and the fact that they barely touched base due to conflicting work schedules. Neither of them was happy about that.

"You were separated for what?" Karen scrunched her face, trying to recall the information. "Four years?"

"Five." Davida shook her head. "I know it's crazy, but things clicked when we saw each other again."

"You sound pretty confident."

"I am," Davida confirmed.

"Good." Karen Kelly studied her friend. "That makes what I have to say easier."

"Okay." Davida stared back. "Should I be concerned?"

"Not necessarily." Karen reached for her file. "It depends on who fathered your child."

"What?"

"You're pregnant."

"About six weeks."

"Pretty much."

"For the record, I never slept with Tom." Davida ignored her raised eyebrow. "I wasn't ready, and Tom didn't know he was waiting for Leslie to break up with her latest squeeze. I think we both wanted us to work when we subconsciously knew we couldn't.

"So, this is Jensen's baby?"

"No question about it," Davida confirmed. "We slipped up on his last visit."

Several times. With hindsight, it would be a shock if she hadn't conceived. She'd consciously stopped taking birth control when she'd returned home for obvious reasons. Less obvious, she felt it would deter her from tumbling into bed with Jensen at the first opportunity. It hadn't.

She'd simply decided it didn't matter if she conceived or not. They'd been married seven years. It didn't matter that they were separated for five of those years. They were back together now, and they'd cleared the air between them. Neither of them was going anywhere.

"Good to know." Karen wiped mock sweat from her forehead. "I was afraid I was about to step in the middle of a huge pile of shite."

"Right." Davida snorted. "Tom's been with Leslie longer than I've been pregnant. Besides, I wouldn't be that casual with a lover."

Karen knew that. She was the one who'd prescribed her birth control. She just didn't know she hadn't needed it.

"Hey, it's happened before." Her doctor gently reminded her. "Birth control doesn't always work."

"It can't work if you don't use it." Davida sassed back. "There wasn't any reason. I wasn't seeing Tom anymore, and Jensen and I had agreed to wait until I came home at the end of the season. We decided it would put less stress on a fragile relationship if we were on the same continent for a while before we got physical."

They'd already waited five years. What were a few more months? Jensen had changed his mind without telling her. As for her, she'd gone along for the ride, and what a glorious ride it was. They'd spent most of his visit making up for lost time. Forget eating or sleeping, neither of them wanted to come up for air.

"You're kidding." Karen shook her head. "I get the thing between you and Tom. You guys started dating right after he was burned by Fiona, and you were still raw from your breakup. Anyone could see neither of you was emotionally available for the longest time."

"I think we both knew it wasn't right from the start," Davida admitted. "But I think we could have made it work if I hadn't run into Jensen again. I also think we would have short-changed each other. Leslie's a much better fit."

"Is Jensen a better fit for you?" Karen's voice bled skepticism. "I know you've passed the point of no return, but whatever imploded your marriage the first go around did a real number on you. Are you sure you want to risk that again?"

"I don't have a choice now." Davida snorted. "Besides, things wouldn't have ended up the way they did if I'd confronted Jensen."

As close as they were, she'd never told Karen what ended her marriage.

"Why didn't you?" Karen asked the obvious.

"I was young and stupid." The classic excuse. "I suppose you want the scoop?"

"Oh, yeah, and I've got time." While not a gossip herself, Karen gladly heard it all. "You're my last patient of the day."

"I figured that." Davida's laugh was genuine. "My dad is the head accountant for the Blakes, so I grew up around the family. While I knew Jensen in passing, we didn't move in the same circles. He's close to fourteen years older than me."

"That's a lot." Especially considering Davi wasn't even thirty. "How did you end up together?"

"We ran into each other at the office." Davida laughed at the look on her friend's face. "It wasn't love at first sight. Far from it. I'd just told him off for not letting my father take me to the airport when I was leaving the country to study abroad."

"You didn't." She knew she had. "You did."

"I did." Davida laughed again. "My dad wasn't happy about that. He was even less pleased when I started dating Jensen. He thought he was too old and too experienced for me. While that was probably true, Jensen never tried to take advantage of me. He was an honorable boyfriend and a better husband."

"Then what happened?" Something catastrophic from Davi's pensive attitude.

"Jensen was engaged before we met," Davida stated matter-of-factly. "Sharon left him a month before their high society wedding for a bigger fish. When that move didn't pay off, she tried to get a do-over. He wasn't interested. Not that he would have been otherwise, but we'd started dating and things were going well."

Karen's disgusted huff spoke volumes.

"She pulled a nasty after you were married." Her doctor didn't have to be a rocket scientist to see where this was going. "And you hit the road instead of talking to your husband."

"Something like that," Davida admitted. "I was going back to confront him about everything when I ended up in the Emergency Room. I had a miscarriage and blamed Jensen, which was stupid. Neither of us knew I was pregnant."

Karen winced at her words.

"He didn't even know what Sharon had done until he returned home to find me gone and my wedding bands on the kitchen counter. I didn't bother leaving a note. I thought the magazine said it all. To make matters worse, I shut down all direct communication after that. We've talked through our lawyers ever since."

"Somehow, that doesn't surprise me." Karen shook her head. "What did Sharon do to make you leave?"

"Engineered a raunchy photograph the rags picked up," Davida admitted. "One that was vulgar and intimate with her hand down his pants in a way it should never be. Adding insult to injury, she made sure the whole world saw it."

The fact that Jensen wasn't impacted in the business sector should have told her something, but it hadn't.

"Why would the gossip rags be interested in your husband?" Karen was beginning to realize her friend was more than the random American archaeologist she thought she was.

"You know that expensive boutique you frequent in London?" The one with the price tags that made her wince. "My mother-in-law owns that whole block."

"You're one of those Blakes." The pieces fell into place. "Your mother-in-law is Tara Blake. From what I hear, she went to visit a great aunt in Hotlanta on vacation and never came back. She married some muckety-muck businessman instead and made her mark in society instead."

Karen laughed at Davida's knowing eye roll. She'd been talking to some overzealous clerk in that over-priced boutique again. The girls working there were proud of their connection to Lady Burton's great niece across the pond.

"The Burtons have owned some musty old estate in the country outside of London for several hundred years. I think her brother has a minor title."

She'd been more interested in shopping than listening to her favorite clerk rattle off the Burton pedigree.

"He does, and my mother-in-law has dual citizenship." While she didn't know much about Tara's family, she did know that much. "I'm assuming your intel came from some gossipy sales associate at your favorite boutique." She laughed softly. "I thought so. Well, your friend knows more than I do in some ways and less in others. Tara never came home because she was interviewing for a job at one of the most prestigious law firms in the city. She got the job, and she landed Dan a couple of years later. While I knew they visited her family in London once or twice a year, I never knew much beyond that."

"I'm sure that will change now that you live here." She'd probably meet the rest of the family if Karen didn't miss her guess, and when she did, Davida was in for a bit of a shock. There was a lot more to her husband's family than she knew. "Now that all of that is out of the way, let's get back to your story. I'm assuming Jensen got wind you were back in the city and blindsided you somehow?"

"You could say that." Davida refused to give up all her secrets. "Let's just say between him and my father, they finally convinced me that I was wrong to leave in the first place. That I owed my marriage a second chance.

I decided they were right. We're still fine-tuning the details, but so far, so good. I think Jensen might try to buy the manor, and I'm fairly sure Seeley will sell."

She hoped he would anyway.

"In a heartbeat." Karen agreed. "He couldn't care less about that old place. He's more interested in money. From the looks of those rings on your finger, price won't be a problem."

"Not if Seeley's reasonable." Unfortunately, the man tended towards greed. "If he isn't, it'll be interesting to see how things play out."

As for Jensen, he'd know what the manor was worth down to the last pound, and he'd have a set price in mind. As condescending and slippery as Seeley could be, he didn't stand a chance. Jensen didn't suffer fools lightly. If anyone could buy the manor, he would.

"I guess it will." Karen looked over her file one last time. "Davi, while I'm sorry about what happened last time, everything looks good right now. I don't think you have anything to worry about this time." Karen put the file away. "From what I can see, you're both healthy. There's nothing to indicate you're at high risk in any way. We'll monitor everything closely to make sure it stays that way. You need to take care of yourself, eat right, and get enough rest. Other than that, just be happy and gestate."

"I'll try." Now that their conversation was winding down, Davida wasn't sure how she felt about this newest twist. "I'll feel better when I see Jensen in a couple of days. He'll be excited enough for both of us."

"I hope you're excited, too." Karen watched her closely. "It's your baby, too."

"I will be when I get my mind around it." Davida nodded. "Right now, I'm amazed it happened so fast. Knowing what might happen and having it happen are two different things."

"I guess it is." Karen agreed since she'd felt that way herself not that long ago.

"We tried unsuccessfully to conceive for a year before we finally decided to take a break. There wasn't any rush, so I went back on birth control, increased my class load, and my philanthropy. We were doing everything right, so I should have been home free. That's one reason I didn't know I was pregnant."

"Girlfriend, we could find a million women out there with a story just like yours." Karen laughed gently. "Me included. We tried for three years before we had Terrence. It didn't help that our tests were normal. When we finally gave up trying, I was pregnant in less than three months. I can't tell you why, but stress probably played a role in there."

"You may be right." Davida suspected she was. "This time, I had already laid down the law about being a baby machine. I'm not doing it. Jensen agreed to let things happen when they happen."

"So, you were just going with the flow." Karen's smile expanded wickedly. "And everything lined up just right for the universe to yell, 'Gotcha!'"

"That's one way of looking at it," Davida growled at her. "The other is less charitable. We bopped like bunnies without protection."

"Don't be a grump." Karen laughed out loud. "You're just frustrated you didn't get to control where and when, but I know you're happy. I can see it in your eyes."

"Yeah, well, my eyes are moving faster than the rest of me." She was truthfully scared witless. "It still doesn't feel real. I think I'll swing by the site and let everyone know we're done until the weather clears before I go home to sit in my window seat and watch the rain fall."

"Sounds like a great idea." Karen rose to her feet. "Give me a call if you need a reality check."

"Don't think I won't." Davida rose to her feet as well. "You're going to have to give me pointers on how to be a working mother. Terry is such a great kid that I know you're doing something right."

"Yeah, well, I think his dad has more to do with that." Karen opened the door. "But I'll help you any way I can. For the record, I think you'll do great without me."

"We'll see." Davida walked out the door. "I'll let you know how Jensen takes the news as soon as I tell him."

Karen laughed out loud at her friend's antics. As funny as that sounded, Davida meant every word she said. She didn't envy the mysterious Jensen dealing with his wife over the coming months. The woman could be a firecracker without the mood swings sure to come.

• • • •

DAVIDA CARRIED HER bag into the house and locked the door behind her. She'd already swung by the site to let her team know they could call it a day. The weather was way too wet to hang out in the mud and the muck like they usually did. They could pick up where they left off when the weather was better. Not surprisingly, everybody was glad to lock things down and go home.

Making a cup of decaf, Davida made a quick sandwich from leftover farm-grown chicken in her fridge. While not the worst thing she could eat since the bread was fresh-baked whole grain, and the veggies were organic, she'd strive to do better in the future. Follow that list of dos and don'ts Karen gave her. Right now, she couldn't even get her mind around the idea of a grocery list, much less write one.

Carrying her lunch to the window seat, she plopped against the wall and stared out over her rain-drenched garden. This was her favorite place to do paperwork on a good day. Unfortunately, this wasn't one of them. A good day. But she could find peace in the beauty outside her window anyway.

While she'd known this was possible, neither she nor Jensen believed it probable. Experience was on their side. She'd been six years younger when they tried before. It had taken over a year for her to conceive then. To their way of thinking, it would take a lot longer this time around. They were wrong. She knew that now in a very concrete way. Resting her palm on her belly, she was mildly surprised she still felt the same. Her skinny pants weren't even tight.

Taking a bite of her sandwich, Davida decided she wasn't sure she was ready to share just yet. Jensen was coming in a couple of days, but that didn't mean she had to tell him. Not yet. Get his hopes up. Maybe she could wait a bit to be sure nothing untoward happened.

He'd be back three or four weeks after that. She'd feel a little more confident by then. From the reading material Karen gave her, she'd probably have a cute little bump by then. One she could show off to his or her best advantage to an unsuspecting dad. After that, she probably wouldn't have to say a word. Jensen would know what he was looking at. With every passing second, that plan was growing on her.

While Karen was reassuring, Davida wasn't confident that history wouldn't repeat itself. She needed time to get her mind around the life cocooned within her. Time to convince herself that nature wouldn't grind her joy into the imaginary sand. Stacking her empty cup on her plate, she carried it to the sink.

As much as she wanted to rush to the nearest phone to call Jensen, she wouldn't. Not yet. She might change her mind later. Right now, she couldn't. As hard as he'd tried to keep a degree of emotional distance between them and what they were doing, she knew better.

This baby was more than the next Blake heir. This little one was a part of him, and he, or she, was desperately loved and wanted. Or they would be if Jensen knew they existed. For all his devotion to Blake, her husband was, and always had been, a loving family man.

Swiping at a tear, Davida wanted to blame her hormones, but the truth was far different. She'd made a terrible mistake. She knew that now. While she'd created her dream career from the ashes of her life, she'd denied herself the love she so desperately wanted and already had for far too many years.

CHAPTER TWENTY-THREE

Grabbing her weekender from the seat, Davida carefully closed the door to her rental car. She was fortunate to find one on such short notice. Then again, short-notice rental cars were a recurring theme in her life recently. Silently unlocking the front door, she dealt with the security system and made her way through the darkness to the half bath.

Closing the door behind her, she flicked the light switch and set her bag on the edge of the tub. Quickly changing in the guest bathroom, she said a silent prayer that Jensen would sleep through her ambush. Leaving the darkened room, she made her way down the hall to the bedroom they'd once shared. She knew he'd moved back into their home soon after she'd returned to England because he'd told her so.

Sliding the door open, she gazed at her husband comfortably splayed across the bed, bathed in silvery moonlight. Some things never change. He was still the same unrepentant bed hog. He probably always would be. Not that she was complaining. Jensen Blake was a sight to behold, bare-chested, wearing nothing but silky pajama pants.

Walking across the room, she quickly slipped into the bed beside him, mildly surprised when Jensen rolled over to face her. He didn't sleep as deeply as he used to anymore. Or he'd been playing possum from the start.

"What are you doing home?" Jensen stroked her hair. "I wasn't expecting you for a few weeks."

"I got an unexpected break," Davida said, touching his cheek. "I missed you, so I decided to come home for a bit."

"You could have called me." Jensen kissed her. "I would have picked you up."

"And ruined the surprise?" Davida chastised him. "I have a rental parked in the driveway."

Her car had been traded in about the time Jensen moved into his condo. It was clear she wasn't coming home anytime soon, so he didn't need a second car. He'd have to remedy that soon. They would need two cars again.

"I'll move it into the garage in the morning." Jensen's hand suddenly paused on her back. "Is this the gown I gave you?"

He'd picked it up in a boutique in London on his last visit.

"What do you think?" Davida laughed softly, feeling his palm stroking sensually against her skin. "You know how I feel about silk."

"I do." Jensen stopped the hands reaching for the waistband of his pajama pants. "You've had a long flight. We can wait."

"Right." Davida snarked. "I can sleep back home."

"So, you're a woman with a mission." Jensen laughed softly. "I've missed you enough to regret letting you stay."

"You didn't have a choice." Davida reminded him. "I didn't ask you to leave Blake. You can't ask me to leave Deira. That's not on the table."

Besides, she'd had a lot to work through over the past few weeks. Things he didn't know about. She'd done that largely by designing the nursery in her downtime. Not that she'd had a lot of that, but when she did, she stayed busy laying out her baby's abode in the small bedroom next to hers. Truthfully, she'd designed two layouts, one for the manor and one for here. Looking through the catalogs, she'd all but decided on the classic Beatrix Potter theme she'd loved as a child for the manor.

She wasn't so sure about Atlanta. She'd finally decided Jensen should probably have a say in that. It was his home, too.

"No, it isn't." Jensen brushed his lips against hers. "Don't worry. I'm not going to try to change the rules now."

"Thank you." Davida agreed. "However, I'm where I belong in the moment."

"Yes, you are." Jensen ran his fingers through her hair. "As long as you're happy, nothing else matters."

"Not exactly." Davida stopped him from kissing her. "There's something you should know."

"Later." Jensen leaned in to capture her lips with his. "We have other things to do."

"Yes, we do." Smirking against his lips, Davida casually straddled his lap, ignoring his pleasured groan. "I've missed you."

"The feeling is mutual." Reaching up to steady her, Jensen suddenly halted their kiss. "About that something that I need to know."

Reaching down to grasp the hand resting on her hip, Davida slowly pressed his palm against the swell of her lower belly.

"We're thirteen weeks and doing well." Davida felt Jensen's hands grip her waist tightly as he digested her words. "I didn't want to tell you over the phone. That's why I came home the first chance I had."

Unexpected business commitments had kept Jensen in Georgia despite their plans. Red tape connected with expanding her dig did the same with Davida. Frustrated by events they couldn't control, they'd postponed their reunion three times. There was no way she was letting that happen again. She'd seized an unexpected break to come home for a few days.

"I know we said we'd be alright no matter what happened, but I never expected this." They'd taken half-hearted precautions after the first time. "I just took it for granted it would take a while."

"So did I," she agreed. "This was the last thing I expected. My doctor assured me this was perfectly normal, and I shouldn't be surprised since we'd done what it takes." Davida laughed at his quirked brow. "Karen is an old friend as well as my doctor. It took her a few minutes to convince me the tests were right, then it knocked me for a loop for a while. I didn't know what to think, so I was glad you were visiting in a few days. Then you weren't."

Their "dates" kept getting disrupted from that point forward. She'd planned to tell him over an intimate dinner at home before he suddenly called to cancel. That happened twice more. Then she'd been about to call an emergency computer call when she'd had a sudden break in her schedule. While the season was winding down, the meetings and paperwork weren't. Fortunately, one of those meetings had been unexpectedly postponed for a week.

"I'm sorry I wasn't able to keep our dinner date." He'd tried everything possible to get to her, but Dan had relapsed in the middle of his already full plate. He'd had no choice but to stay close in case the worst happened. Fortunately, it hadn't, and his father was stable and back in remission for the present. And I'm sorry to have lost six weeks with both of you."

"Seven, but who's counting?" She was. Every minute that she couldn't tell him what he needed to know. While she'd doubted her decision, she'd made a judgment call. "I thought this was an announcement better made in person. I'm sorry if you feel differently."

"I don't," he agreed with her. "While I wish things were different, knowing all the moments I was missing would have driven me nuts."

He rested his palm against her belly, imagining what lay beneath her skin.

"Good." Davida closed her eyes briefly. "I was scared you'd be angry."

"Never." This felt surreal. "Do you know what we're having?"

"I do," Davida admitted. "I had blood tests to check for abnormalities."

"And?" He absently traced circles on her hand.

"Do you want to know?" She laughed softly at his impatient nod. "Okay. Then we'll make Dan's day."

"He won't care either way." Jensen wasn't sure if he was happy to be having the coveted Blake heir or sad not to get a sassy girl like her mom. Probably a little of both. "Mom won't either. They're just happy we're back together and hope they'll get that first grandchild sooner rather than later."

It wouldn't surprise him if his parents eventually decided it didn't matter if a male or a female headed Blake Enterprises anymore. While that was irrelevant if what Davi said was true, he hoped they were getting more in step with the times. If he had a daughter capable of running the business, he wouldn't hesitate to hand the reins to her when the time came, if he was allowed to.

"I'm sure that's exactly what they tell you every Thursday night over dinner." Davida laughed softly. "At least the grandchild part."

"And you would be right." Jensen agreed. "They'll be thrilled."

"I guess they will." Davida rested her palm against his chest. "Then we'll invite them to dinner and share the news before I leave." She was far enough along to be comfortable doing that. "As crazy as this sounds, there's something about telling you that makes this feel more real."

"It's real all right." Jensen rested his hand on top of hers. "I couldn't be happier."

He was ecstatic, considering this was the last thing he expected when he opened his eyes to see someone creeping through the darkness towards his bed. While that should have startled him, he'd instantly recognized Davi in the moonlight streaming through the half-open blinds. Besides, their home was in a luxury gated community with security patrols and a top-of-the-line security system. Considering who lived in this neighborhood, he slept well at night.

"I'm glad." Davida blinked. "Five years ago, I would have taken this in stride. Now, it's rocked my world. I've spent so long convincing myself this would never happen; I can't get my mind around the fact it has."

"I get it," Jensen reassured her. "I'm having trouble of my own."

"I guess you are." Davida laughed. "It's not like I didn't wake you up in the middle of the night to spring the p-word on you."

"Yeah, well, you can do that any time you'd like." Jensen pulled her against him. "Maybe not the p-word part, but the rest, you better believe it."

"Sounds like a plan." Davida closed her eyes. "I'm scared witless this is going to blow up in our faces, but I'm excited, too."

"Yeah?" That was good. "Are you ready to be a mother?"

"Getting there." Davida rested her hand on her belly. "I'm far enough along to believe everything will be okay."

But not necessarily far enough to believe she'd be a good mother. Once upon a time, she'd been convinced she'd be great with that youthful conviction that she could do anything she turned her mind to. That included finishing her doctorate while being Mother of the Year. It seemed the perfect blend of personal and professional goals at the time. Right. She was older and wiser now.

"Good." Jensen's slightly dazed smile lit up his face. "Then we'll work out the rest as we go along."

Nodding, Davida decided she liked the look on him. Turning the tables and knocking Jensen off kilter for a change was empowering. Slightly gob-smacked looked good on him. Laughing softly, she pulled her gown over her head as she smoothly shoved him back on the bed. If her husband thought he was the only one who could have his wicked way, he was in for a rude awakening. She had needs, too.

EPILOGUE

A tlanta, Georgia, USA
Looking around the small bonus room across from their bedroom, Davida decided it was about the same size as the nursery back home. While she was positive about the Beatrix Potter theme at the manor, she was leaning more towards a dinosaur theme stateside. She'd seen several interesting ideas online to use for inspiration. All she had to do was get Jensen on board. He was fine with the menagerie of bunnies, ducks, and hedgehogs she wanted for back home. He'd probably be fine with the dinos here. She'd run the idea by him in the car.

Glancing at her watch, she shook her head as she walked across the hall to the master bath. Slicking gloss over her lips, Davida crammed the slender tube in her back pocket as she headed for the stairs. Gathering her resolve, she prepared to give her husband a strong shoulder to lean on. He would need it before they were done.

Both of their worlds had crumbled earlier this morning when Jensen called his parents to invite them to an intimate dinner by the pool. So much for best-laid plans. Ones that ended with a custom carrot cake decorated with a blue, floppy-eared bunny holding a yellow baby rattle. Sadly, that dinner wouldn't happen anytime soon. If at all.

Unbeknownst to anyone but his wife, Dan had opted for a radical new treatment in a last-ditch effort to save his life. As risky as it was, Tara supported his choice. It was a glimmer of hope in an otherwise desperate situation. She was the one who'd finally shared what he'd done with them. That was why she and Jensen were headed for a well-known cancer treatment center instead of the nearest grocery store.

"Are you good to go?" Davida held out the car keys. "I can drive if you'd like."

Jensen still looked a little misty-eyed and shaky, even if he'd deny it. As much as she preferred to ride, she'd gladly drive if he needed her to.

"That's not necessary." Jensen took the keys and kissed her cheek. "I'm fine. From what Mom said, the worst is over."

"Okay." Davida pecked his lips. "I'll trust your judgment."

"Then grab your sweater and we'll go." Jensen followed her out the door, amused that she had her driver's license and a credit card in that little RFID holder stuck on the phone in her back pocket. "You're not taking your purse?"

"You know better than that." While she used a purse when necessary, she preferred not to when it wasn't. "I have everything I need in my back pocket."

"And your lipstick crammed in my front pocket." He laughed softly when she shoved the small tube of color exactly where he'd expected. "That's what I thought."

He opened the door for her and fastened her seat belt before closing the door behind her.

"Yeah, well, what's the point in wearing a blousy top if you can't hide your sins?" She watched him pull out of the garage with familiar ease.

"Nothing, I guess." Jensen agreed, patting her hand. "I like that blouse, by the way."

It was either new or one she brought from England since he'd never seen it before. Merging into rush hour traffic, their small talk gradually petered out as he concentrated on driving.

It wasn't that long before they found themselves in the hospital parking lot. A few minutes later, they were standing outside an ICU hospital room.

"You ready?" Davida brushed imaginary lint from Jensen's suit jacket. "It's going to be okay."

"I should be reassuring you." Jensen stroked her hair. "But thank you. Let's do this before I lose my nerve."

Watching him open the door, Davida walked through, knowing Jensen was doing his best to ignore the beeping machines and IV stands. While Tara had warned them that Dan would look like death warmed over, seeing him looking so gray was unnerving. She'd never seen his color so bad. When she'd last seen him at their reconciliation dinner, he'd looked far better than expected.

However, the fact that Dan survived the treatment itself was a good sign that he'd pull through. If he did, his quality and quantity of life would be greatly improved at the worst. At best, he might be in complete remission. One they hoped was permanent.

"Hey, Dad," Jensen spoke softly. "We have some news for you."

"Yeah?" Dan opened his eyes to see Davida sitting in a chair with Jensen standing guard behind her. "What's so important that you had to wake me up?"

That final round of treatment was hell. He still had trouble opening his eyes and keeping them open three days later. The last thing he needed was having his beauty sleep interrupted. Not now that he was on the cusp of getting that cure, although the old fogeys would never use that word. Anyway, his doctors were beyond pleased with his progress, and he was looking forward to moving on with his life. To going home to Tara, where he belonged.

"I'm pregnant." Davida reached out to take his hand. "So, you have another reason to fight this thing."

"You're kidding me?" Dan squeezed her hand. "How far along?"

"Fourteen weeks." Davida felt Jensen's hand on her shoulder. "And healthy as a horse."

"Good to know." Dan raised his bed to a sitting position. "Then you're staying together. No more running off to the other side of the world instead of tackling your problems?"

Davida's look said it all.

"And no more burying your pain in high rent..." Dan caught himself. "Opportunists that you don't care two cents about?"

Jensen choked on his spit as Dan said how he truly felt. He'd forgotten how brutally honest the other man could be. Fortunately, his father chose a little restraint out of respect for Davida. While he'd mellowed considerably during his illness, he hadn't lost his fire. He was still the strong, opinionated man he'd always admired and loved.

"While I think they'd object to being characterized that way," his father's rude eye roll said it all. "I won't be seeing other women. We're back together for good. Davi wouldn't be pregnant if we weren't."

"Smart girl." Dan patted her hand. "You'd let my sorry son lose everything before you'd compromise your values."

Dan didn't know Jensen had spilled the beans that the threat was off the table, so Davida decided to play along. She'd act surprised when he finally told her himself. What he didn't know wouldn't hurt him. It might even make for a good laugh down the road.

"She would," Jensen agreed. "Dad, you should know this child isn't something we take lightly. We'd like a couple more before we're done."

"Since I don't think either of your sisters intends to procreate, I like your plan." Jensen thought he was playing, but he wasn't.

One daughter had no interest in motherhood, and the other had no interest in men. She was much too busy with her startup to have time for romance. While that might change, he didn't count on it. Not any time soon. Right now, she was content to casually mix business with pleasure with her financial advisor. As they were both single adults, there wasn't anything he could say about it. Besides, his girls knew what they wanted. They also knew they could do as they pleased. The brunt of the family's expectations rested on their big brother.

"I think three is a nice number, but I also think I'd like to see you with two boys and a girl for a change."

"And I think we'll take what we get and be happy." Davida laughed at Dan's large and in charge attitude. "I think you will, too."

"You know me too well." Dan reached out to take her hand. "How my son ever let you get away in the first place is beyond me. So, son, it only took you five months to get the job done." Dan's look said it all. "He's always been a little slow on the follow-through. His mom was already knocked up before we got back from the honeymoon."

Davida blushed. She so didn't need to know that. No way. Then again, that manly swagger was so Dan. It was nice to see his illness hadn't beaten the cocky out of him. He was still the same brash, occasionally crass, man she'd known and loved all her life.

"It's kind of hard to conceive when you're not on the same continent, so I think you should cut him some slack." Davida good-naturedly chastised her father-in-law. "You know I was in England while Jensen was here during the first few months of our reconciliation."

"You have a point there." Dan conceded. "However, that doesn't account for that four-day layover he took on the way home from Edinburgh, oh, say, about fourteen weeks ago."

Davida shot her husband a dirty look, ignoring the hastily raised palms protesting his innocence.

"I didn't say anything." Jensen shook his head in defeat. "You have my word."

"He didn't have to." Dan snorted. "That spark he'd been missing was back. I knew you'd sealed the deal without Jensen saying a word."

He smirked at his son in that condescending way he despised.

"Since there was also a pub receipt from your village buried in his paperwork, I knew exactly where he was while he was off the grid. Where, and with whom. It didn't take a rocket scientist to figure out the two of you were finally taking care of business. While I didn't expect this outcome so soon, I knew you were back together the way you should be."

Davida shook her head in disbelief. She should have known Dan would know everything going on at Blake. His mind was too sharp to retire and take up a hobby. He was business through and through. He'd taken the company to new heights during his tenure, largely because of that never-stop attitude. Things weren't about to change since he retired. Or because of a serious illness.

"Dad, that's enough." Jensen rested his hand on Davida's shoulder. "Davi can't get any redder."

Dan laughed softly, enjoying the pink dusting her cheeks. Her father's misstep aside, David was a good man, and he'd raised a good kid. One that he was proud to call family. While he was sad for the time lost, the couple before him was better off for their separation.

Davida had come into her own over the last five years, and Jensen realized love wasn't everything. He needed to value his wife's hopes and dreams as much as his own. Protect and nurture them. From what he could see, their relationship was stronger after the mistakes they'd made.

Looking at his son, Dan finally asked the question he should have asked first. "Does your mother know?"

"Not yet. We're meeting her at the club for brunch along with Marti and David." Jensen rested his hand on Davida's shoulder. "We wanted to tell you first."

"Good." Dan closed his eyes briefly. "Tara needs a break. Last night was the first time she left my side since this started. I'm glad you're making a family outing of it. She'll enjoy seeing David and Marti. Tell them hello for me."

She'd been afraid to leave. Afraid he'd die if she did. Tara wasn't entirely wrong. He'd hit several rough spots along the way, but he'd pulled through. While he still had an uphill fight ahead of him, Dan was confident he'd make it, especially with this latest news to egg him on.

"From what Mom told us, she had a good reason for being here," Jensen revealed that they were up to speed on his condition. "I'm glad you're doing better. I just wish I'd known what you were doing. I would have been here, too."

"I know, Son." Dan reached out to grasp his hand. "But you're here now, and that's what I wanted. You had enough on your plate without worrying about your old man."

"I did." Jensen agreed. "But I should have been here for you and Mom."

"You needed to be at Blake protecting the family interests." Dan looked him straight in the eyes. "Jensen, the truth is nobody expected me to make it, and it's a bad way to go. I didn't want you watching me die slowly and painfully to be your last memory of your father."

Jensen nodded. "I respect that."

"I knew you would." Dan's smile was tired. "As happy as I am to see you, I'm running out of steam. I sleep a lot, but they tell me that I'm supposed to. They claim it helps with the healing."

"We have to meet Mom in a few minutes anyway." Jensen wrapped his arm around Davida. "We'll see you tonight if that's okay."

Bring him a slice of that blue bunny cake to celebrate. They'd already cleared it with his nurse.

"I'd like that." Dan patted Davida's hand. "You take care of yourself and my grandson, and don't take any garbage off that one. If he gives you any trouble, call me. I have ways of keeping him in line."

"I'll do that." Davida leaned over to kiss his forehead. "We'll see you tonight."

For all his rough mannerisms, her father-in-law was an honorable, generous man. He was highly regarded, even by his enemies, for good reason. While he could be ruthless, he didn't lie, cheat, or steal. Dan seized opportunities when they became available. If he happened to get there first or outbid the competition, that was due to experience and talent. Not underhanded business practices. Despite his tough exterior, Dan would be a real softie where his grandchild was concerned. Letting Jensen usher her to the door, she watched him smile before uttering a soft, "Later," as they exited the room.

"I know he looks bad." Davida rested a comforting hand on his arm. "But your mom says he's doing well."

"Yeah, she did." Jensen led her down the hall to the elevator. "I'm going to take her word for it."

Hers and the nurse practitioner who was managing his case.

"I think that's a good idea." Davida glanced at her watch. "Oh, man, we need to get a move on."

"It's okay." Jensen crammed his phone back in his pocket before hitting the down button. "Mom just texted she's running about ten minutes late. Amy broke up with her boyfriend and needed a shoulder to cry on."

Ah. The daughter that Dan said was more interested in her company than she was in men. Maybe he was wrong. Things weren't as casual as they seemed. It sounded like she may have had more than a passing interest in her boyfriend.

"She deliberately misrepresented the seriousness of their relationship to my parents for obvious reasons. Now the lie is out. At least to mom. It seems Amy walked in on Ian in bed with another woman. They weren't ready for the altar, but they were monogamous. Or she thought they were. It seems my sister was wrong, and Ian was stupid. Especially considering they exchanged keys several years ago."

Davida made a mental note to call her sister-in-law for a lunch date before she flew home. Amy would appreciate the moral support. She'd appreciate reconnecting with an old friend. One who'd always been in their corner.

"My sister has already pulled her portfolio from Ian's firm. I'm pretty sure it's an account he can't afford to lose, but I support her decision. They dated a couple of years before they mixed business with pleasure, so it wasn't a casual thing from the start. I thought they'd get married when things settled down with the business and Amy came up for air. That won't happen now, so I guess I was wrong." Jensen glanced at his watch. "We can still make it on time if we hurry."

Nodding, Davida stepped into the elevator and pushed the down button. She couldn't wait to see Tara's reaction to their news. If she didn't miss her guess, she'd be more excited than Dan was. Smiling softly, she rested her hand on her belly. She didn't even want to think about her dad or Marti.

"You know, J.J. will have the best grandparents ever."

"Yes, he will." Jensen agreed, cringing that she was already calling their son "J.J." in her mind. "On both sides."

Guiding her out of the elevator, he silently vowed there was no way in heaven or hell Jensen Daniel Blake, Jr, would ever be called "J.J." By anyone. Ever. However, he wisely kept his mouth shut. Considering they had a lot to celebrate, that was a fight for another day.

Don't miss out!

Visit the website below and you can sign up to receive emails whenever Tori Lennox publishes a new book. There's no charge and no obligation.

https://books2read.com/r/B-A-SKFX-UMIHC

BOOKS 2 READ

Connecting independent readers to independent writers.

Did you love *Tattered Promises*? Then you should read *Razor's Edge*[1] by Tori Lennox!

Cassandra Montgomery made her name as a prosecutor, but after threats and a brutal divorce, she rebuilt her life in divorce law. When a powerful enemy frames her for murder, the justice system she once trusted turns against her. On the brink of arrest, she's pulled into the shadows by Keith Neil — a hardened undercover cop who's spent five years infiltrating the same criminal network now hunting them both.

Forced into hiding, Cassie and Neil navigate a deadly web of lies, betrayal, and buried evidence. Every step draws them deeper into a conspiracy that reaches from police precincts to political offices to the very law firm where Cassie once worked. Their uneasy alliance sparks a dangerous connection neither expected, but survival comes first — and the people protecting this empire have already proven they'll do whatever it takes to keep it intact.

The man behind the frame job is watching — and he'll kill again to keep his secrets buried.

Also by Tori Lennox

The Golden Wolf Series Book 2
Back from the Shadowlands

The Golden Wolf Series Book One
The Wolf and the Warrior

The Shards of Promise
Tattered Promises

Standalone
A Necessary Convenience
Toxic Illusions
Razor's Edge
A Particle of Scandal

About the Author

Tori Lennox has always preferred reading to sleeping. With a love for all genres of romance, she enjoys writing both contemporary and historical romances, Originally from South Carolina, Tori now lives in Florida. When she isn't writing, she enjoys cooking, gardening, and walks with her toothless blue and tan dachshund, Mir.